# The Monster of Loon Lake

## THE SHORES OF LOON LAKE

RACHELLE PAIGE CAMPBELL

*Chapter One*

Deep, dark, and disturbed.

Seth Boyd leaned over the tour boat's railing and stared down into the bottomless water of Lake Superior's southern shore. He'd long theorized that this very spot was the sanctuary for a mythical—and all too real—creature he'd hunted since childhood. Over the past six months, the legend had transformed him from small-town printshop owner to minor internet sensation.

His self-published memoir, about his search for Soupy, the Lake Superior monster, had taken off thanks to social media. He'd long hoped once others learned about his hunt, he'd find a community of enthusiasts eager to engage. Everyone wanted a little magic. And he was in the position of sparking some wizardry, no wand required. Sharing his journey, including his successes and failures, connected his very particular mission with the broader world. Or, at least, that was what the morning TV news anchor said. He wasn't sure if she meant it or just read it off the teleprompter.

The attention couldn't steal his focus. He wouldn't let

anything deter him, ever. And especially not on a day like today, when the surface of the water was calm. Under a bright-blue sky, nothing seemed amiss. If an ancient beast could survive for millennia and remain hidden, these coordinates had to be the spot. Seth had dubbed the location the Timber Triangle. The area wreaked havoc on magnetic fields and had destroyed many nautical—and technological—devices. Storms popped up in the local area with sudden, shocking severity. A shipwreck had recently been located, and its treasure, a shipment of whole timbers logged during the nineteenth century now worth a hefty six figures, had been recovered.

On a clear day, the lake was picturesque and still as glass. He had an unobstructed view into the water. But it was fathoms deep, and visibility didn't extend far at this spot. He waited, willing a sighting. The mosasaurus did not surface.

"Until next time, friend," he murmured into the wind, turning away from the microphone he held.

The tour boat began its turn back into the channel leading to Loon Lake, the tiny offshoot of the greatest body of freshwater in the world. The tight-knit community along the shore survived and thrived during its hundred-plus years of existence because of its fundamental belief in caring for each other like family. Now, during the summer's big 150th celebration, that pride and spirit were on full display.

He faced the eager crowd of tourists and raised the microphone. "Sorry, folks. Soupy prefers overcast skies. But don't let our uneventful tour deter you from your own sightings." He pointed to the log cabin at the top of a hill. "Our museum is a prime spot for observation, as is the newly reopened sawmill." He swung his arm to the other side of the lakeshore.

"If Soupy is in the lake, wouldn't he be too large to hide?" A woman called.

Squinting, Seth spotted the lady near the railing. With a

baseball cap pulled low, her features were hidden. Obscured from view. Like a certain lake monster.

"An interesting question. Yes, a mosasaurus could reach up to fifty feet in length. Some major motion pictures exaggerated the size difference between man and reptile," he said into the microphone, running a hand through his shaggy blond hair.

The tour group chuckled in unison.

"But other smaller mosasaurs called Phosphorosaurus, theorized to be diurnal hunters in deep water, are another option."

"What do you think about the wormhole theory?" A man asked, shouting.

A few in the crowd sniggered and shook their heads.

Seth wanted to encourage, not dismiss, the outlandish question outright. He didn't mind wild asks. Interacting with folks was a highlight of the tours, and he hoped his responses showed his respect and appreciation. But at the moment, he was drawing a blank. "The wormhole theory?" he repeated, stalling for a few seconds.

"Yeah, like a shortcut between the modern world and ancient times," the man explained.

Since appearing on a national morning TV show, Seth had been inundated with tips and theories on his website. Most recently, a podcast theorized that the presence of quartz and other minerals indicated the potential for time travel. "I have heard it. Our shores are rich with mineral deposits, including granite. It remains a possibility, but I suspect the prevalence of iron ore and copper inhibits any rips in the space-time continuum. And I think the distance between the shores prevents a Casimir plate from occurring."

The man nodded.

Seth had only begun leading tours of the lake a few weeks ago and was open to all suggestions. Thus far, he'd heard only positive reviews. He loved sharing his passion with interested people, and the response encouraged him.

"Back in the day," Seth said. "Strange occurrences were reported with some regularity. Fish populations have boomed. Odd waves were spotted near the mouth of the channel. It wasn't until I started logging what I had seen that an official record was established."

A young boy raised his hand.

"Yes?" Seth asked.

The boy jumped to his feet. "My dad says back in the day means the nineties."

A collective chuckle sounded on the deck.

Seth smiled. "Yes. Back in the day means the nineties for some. For me, I'm talking about the early years of this new millennium."

"I saw a shark," the boy said. He pointed toward the railing behind Seth with animation, bouncing on the balls of his feet. "Could Soupy be a shark?"

Seth appreciated the kid's enthusiasm and hated to burst his bubble. "Sharks can't live in freshwater lakes. It's a good idea but impossible. You might have seen a large fish."

The boat slowed as it neared the dock.

"Thank you again for your time and attention. I am happy to welcome all of you into the Society of Soupy. You are hereby inducted and honorarily deputized to conduct your own scientific research. Remember to report anything unusual via the online form."

The crowd clapped.

Seth bowed, hiding his flushed cheeks for a second. He wasn't used to receiving attention. Life in a small town meant never really standing out or surprising anyone. That was okay. He wasn't a flashy, look-at-me person. But he didn't shy away from what his newfound fame had done—and could do.

Getting answers about the elusive beast became more of a

possibility with every article and interview. Finding Soupy was his life's work. After first spotting the animal during a reluctant ice fishing outing with his dad nearly thirty years ago, Seth had devoted himself to research and study. Until passing a few years earlier, Dad had been his partner. Now, with the new tips and theories, Seth was sure he'd solve the mystery.

He turned off the microphone and made his way to the back of the boat. Shaking hands and posing for pictures, he bid every person goodbye. With a sell-out tour, that was no small feat.

"Great job today," Grant Reem, the tour boat owner, said, making his way through the departing crowd on the dock and hopping on board. "We're sold out of the official merch at the gift shop."

"Wow, that's great news. I'm heading to the printshop. I'll make another run of... everything," Seth said.

Taking over his family's business didn't distract from his real goal. If anything, running a printshop enhanced his work with Soupy. He'd started merchandising with stickers as a way to fund his hunt. Gasoline for his skiff, binoculars, cameras, various sonar and listening devices—all of which had broken and been replaced over the years—weren't free. He hadn't secured any corporate sponsors despite his best efforts. But his search and funding really took off after his story went viral. Donations poured in to help.

Murmured voices cut through the silence.

Grant scanned over Seth's shoulder. "Is someone still on board?"

Seth shook his head. "I think the noise is coming from your pants."

"Oops." Grant fumbled for his phone in his front pocket. "Sorry. I was listening to a podcast." With a sigh, he turned off the device. "I hope the search for Soupy goes on forever." Grant chuckled. "Good for my business."

Seth forced a smile. Grant's words chilled Seth. Dying without answers was Seth's nightmare. He prayed—fervently—the other man hadn't cursed the hunt. He had to discover the truth to cement his family's legacy in a town chock full of history. Only Soupy—the mosasaurus—would do. Otherwise, the Boyds would be a nameless part of the past, subservient to other, bigger families. Seth owed Dad a legacy.

"Speaking of business, I'd better get back to my store," Seth said.

"I'll catch you tonight at Molly's event?"

"I wouldn't miss it." With a wave, Seth exited the boat and strolled down the dock. His slip-on loafers slapped every board, the soundtrack to his whirring thoughts.

Grant had purchased the tour boat company almost a year earlier. While he owned one of the oldest businesses, he was a relative newcomer. Along with his girlfriend, Molly Maguire, who had inherited the old sawmill and been the rightful owner of the sunken logs in the lake, Grant was learning the unspoken ways of the town.

Seth scanned the lakeshore as he reached solid ground. Just past the boathouse, a grand Victorian resort rose through the pines. Nestled on a beach boasting a rebuilt, non-functional, probably haunted lighthouse, the Inn at Loon Lake practically founded the town devoted to tourism. The Hales realized the potential for catering to visitors rather than industry. They bought land and built a boardwalk of shops and eateries for their guests, leased to tenants but still owned in the present day by the inn.

Seth pounded the wooden sidewalk of the boardwalk shops most days, dropping off print orders and restocking copies of *Loon Lake Life*, the local paper he published. Most of the businesses in town had been family-owned for generations, passing from parent to child. While the inn's management had temporarily threatened the arrangement by valuing profits over people, the return of a Hale to the property resolved the animosity brewing between the businesses.

Reaching the parking lot, Seth hopped into his car and turned over the engine, heading towards his store, a short drive away in a strip mall off the main highway into town. The spot wasn't picturesque, but it was quiet, and he owned the store outright. Something to be very grateful for.

The influx of tourists, thanks to Soupy's popularity, was an accomplishment he claimed. He had done his part to increase awareness of Loon Lake before the start of the all-important celebration year. He hoped Elise McKenna, the town's one-woman tourism board, PR contact, and historical society chief, was pleased. All he had to do now was deliver a monster, and he'd secure his place in town lore.

Easy, peasy.

* * *

Elise McKenna hated surprises. It wasn't just the shock of the unknown that distressed her. She was offended by the most basic definition of the word. Unexpected.

That was too kind to encapsulate exactly how off-putting, troublesome, and chaotic any situation that involved the purposeful shock of another. More like unwarranted. Unwelcome. Any other number of un- starting words.

She preferred order and reason.

If others called her emotionless, she didn't care. With an eye on the past and her mind on the future, she was nothing more than a steward of her beloved hometown. In her roles as manager of the tourism board and president of the historical society, she answered to the town at a yearly budget meeting. Otherwise, she operated alone. Just the way she liked it. Lately, however, she couldn't seem to avoid the unexpected or working with others.

"Earth to Elise?" Ashley Hale-Lewis snapped her fingers. "Is that a yes or a no on jumping out of a cake?"

Elise didn't expend the energy to roll her eyes at the woman she'd known since kindergarten.

"Okay, scratch that off the list." Ashley jotted down something on her clipboard. "Molly, you said the staff set up the tables yesterday?"

Molly nodded her head across the table.

The trio sat in the corner of the Inn at Loon Lake's restaurant. A few diners joined them, but most of the guests enjoyed the beautiful day outdoors on the patio.

Elise was glad for the relative peace. Tonight's big event was an important first step to securing the town's history in perpetuity. Not that either of the women who'd expressed their desire to help understood the seriousness to Elise.

"What time will catering arrive?" Molly asked. She had graciously opened her recently restored family sawmill to Elise for the sesquicentennial kickoff.

The paid admission event was the first fundraiser to help establish a trust for the museum, ensuring its continuation. Twelve months ago, she had come to appreciate how—despite her best efforts—she didn't have all the answers or know what was coming next. Elise's close friendship with Molly's great aunt, Lily Maguire, secured the town's foundation as the heir to the sawmill if Molly couldn't be located. Elise had tricked herself into thinking of the inheritance as a given. For years, she hadn't taken action to prepare for the future. She refused to be passive in her professional—and personal—life any longer. Controlling every variable was impossible. But she'd do her best to try.

The town's stories must endure.

She thought of herself as a Medieval tradesperson, working on a grand cathedral she'd never see to completion. To that end, she needed funds. Repairs had not been made on the log cabin, which served as the town museum and historical society, for years. The admission fees barely kept the power on. She wouldn't draw a salary, but the next person in her role might. She wanted to show up to the budget meeting in January with a fully funded department.

"All set then?" Ashley pushed back her chair.

"What? Wait, please, I'm sorry." Elise scrubbed her hands over her face. "I was...."

"Worrying again?" Molly offered with a kind smile.

Elise hated to acknowledge the truth. Over the past year, however, she'd learned that both of these women responded to honesty and a little vulnerability. She nodded. "I can't help it. Losing the sawmill solidified how precarious the historical society's situation is. This event has to raise money. Everything that comes next has to reinforce how significant the historical society is to the town and vice versa."

"You have done a fantastic job with the events for the whole summer. Tonight is more about locals realizing how vital our collective stories are. It's a good way to start," Ashley said, scooting her chair closer to the table. "But don't put so much pressure on yourself. Everyone will want to do their part. You're not alone."

Elise hoped Ashley was right. She had filed paperwork to turn the historical society and museum into a full-fledged charity. Her plan was simple. Start with a big splash and keep the momentum going over the months so her year-end requests weren't a shock to the system.

"What's left on your checklist? Are you going home to get ready?" Molly asked.

"Not quite yet," Elise said. "I'm heading to the museum to fetch Mrs. Fitz-Ash and then have a stop at the printshop for an order."

"Ooooh," Ashley said, dragging the word.

"Who?" Molly asked at the same moment.

Elise's cheeks burned. "Seth."

"No, not him. I know Seth," Molly said. "He's leading a tour right now for Grant. Who is Mrs. Fitz-Ash?"

Elise wasn't sure if she was more embarrassed about clarifying Seth unnecessarily, and perhaps drawing attention again to her closeness with him, or Mrs. Fitz-Ash. "She's a... tree. Or sapling. I took a seed pod from the original Ash tree in front of the log cabin and successfully grew a sapling in the year before the tree had to be cut down after borer got it."

"Why Mrs. Fitz-Ash?" Molly asked.

"Sort of a playful nod to all the illegitimate children of British royalty." And because she needed to give the plant a name once it became the friend she talked to the most. With real, living, age-appropriate acquaintances in Molly, Ashley, and Seth, Elise hadn't needed to share quite as much with Mrs. Fitz-Ash. Which might have been how she'd outgrown her pot inside the log cabin before Elise even noticed.

"We don't want to keep you from either that or seeing Seth," Ashley said.

Elise didn't react. She liked Seth. Everyone knew it, and most people liked him, too. The trouble was, she had romantic feelings for him. He was sweet, and kind, and handsome. When she was with him, she liked the person she became.

But she worried he was too good for her. Too amenable with his shining emerald eyes and easy smile. Too handsome despite his blond hair always needing a trim. She had the sense other people talked about how odd the pairing was. That the stoic, serious Elise should spend time with open, easy Seth. That she was somehow taking advantage of him. She'd spent too many hours mentally circling the same arguments. And yet, she couldn't stop herself from seeking him out. Maybe she couldn't give in to her feelings completely, but she didn't want to be denied his company.

"If you'll both excuse me, I'll see you this evening?" Elise stood, gathering her purse off the table.

"I'd better get going, too. Can't wait for the big event," Molly added.

"Thank you for coming to me. We'll have to keep working together so I can return the favor and stop by your businesses," Ashley said with a smile.

Elise nodded and saw herself out. Better to make a slightly rude exit than to stick her foot in her mouth somehow. Ashley was clever and charming. Every defect in Elise was an asset in the other woman. As kids, they'd always rubbed each other wrong, foils to one another. As adults, their longstanding history accounted for more than every tiny slight in their past.

Outside the inn, Elise stalked toward the museum. Climbing up a hill through the forest, she leaped over the trickling stream dug by the original owners of the cabin to empty into a small pond. While the body of water was no longer used for its original purpose, sewage, she avoided it. Unpleasant smells—a noxious mix of weeds, rotting vegetation, and something else she couldn't quite place—were enough to encourage distance. She reached the clearing, and the timber structure came into view.

A cool breeze rustled the leaves of the Aspens surrounding the log cabin. June in the upper Midwest wasn't particularly warm and was definitely not beachy. Which suited Elise.

She'd lived in the area her whole life, never staying south of Wisconsin for long. It was too much. Too many people. Too hot. She liked the cooler climate although she knew that wasn't the reason she'd been called the town ice queen. Her reserved unnerved some people. She found the moniker funny. If the off-putting nickname kept away noisy, gossipy people, she was glad for it.

A mechanical whirring echoed off the hills.

The tour boat passed in the lake. The noise was a cacophony on the otherwise still air.

She raised a hand to shield her gaze against the bright sun and spotted Seth on the side of the boat, holding a microphone and holding court. He was in his element. She smiled, warmth curling low in her belly.

She was glad for him to have a moment of success and the spotlight. In their tiny town, people were categorized early and never had much chance to surprise and shine. She didn't care about such things for herself.

Her work was bigger, looking at the town's founding and every generation since.

But it mattered to Seth.

Since self-publishing his memoir, *Searching for Soupy*, he'd gone viral and thrived under the spotlight. She knew he viewed the attention as positive but what if he became a joke? He never suspected ulterior motives or heard the edge in another's cutting words. He took the world at face value, always finding joy and delight in the people he encountered. He'd never met a stranger.

She had been relieved when the national morning show had focused on the father-son bonding angle rather than the invented myth. While the town started the summer season with a bigger crowd than usual, most tourists wanted to interact with the man and not the monster. The only boats in the lake were those of the tour company. The recently rebuilt and reopened lighthouse wasn't overrun with cameras and sonar equipment. No major monster-hunting outfit had come to their shores.

She had her own theory, mostly that if an unexpected species was in the lake, it was probably an overgrown eel or some sort of pet that had been released and thrived in the wild. Mosasaurus was the last creature she'd suspect. Until Seth had declared one lived in the water, she hadn't known about the extinct species. Suddenly, everyone talked about Soupy.

The visitors wanted to meet Seth.

She'd fielded many questions about him during her tours of the museum. Was he as nice as he seemed? Did he and his dad really spend their ice fishing time drilling holes to look for Soupy? Had anyone ever gone with him on a search?

She knew about the sell-out boat trips he led, too. She was happy. He had his notoriety in a relatively safe way. He was protected. She could relax. And focus.

She grabbed Mrs. Fitz-Ash, lifting with her legs and hauling the heavy pot to her car, still parked in front of the log cabin. She hadn't worried about visitors spotting her vehicle and being upset that the museum was closed and the door locked. If anything, she hoped her car acted as a deterrent. Molly and Grant had entered the museum a year earlier, while she'd stepped out, and damaged a baseboard. Since then, she'd taken security more seriously.

Most of the museum's visitors stopped by after Seth told them to at the end of his tour, but he'd promised he wouldn't mention it today. After securing the plant, she headed back to the building, walking the perimeter to check for trash before she left.

The crunch of tires on the gravel road echoed like fireworks.

A car pulled to a stop on the drive some yards behind hers.

The white sedan looked a little battered in the way of rental cars. Nothing was horribly amiss with the vehicle, but there were scratches on the bumper, as if the driver had misjudged parking spots.

She sucked in a breath. She hoped the driver wouldn't misjudge her museum's parking lot and cause damage. She didn't have any civic funds to repair the log cabin or its land-scaping. Yet.

A man and a woman exited the car.

"Hello," the man called with a smile. Dressed in a polo and khakis, he had a stale look about him.

Elise pressed her lips together and nodded.

"Are you closed?" The woman asked. With shoulder-length hair neatly combed behind her ears and dressed in a sweatshirt and khakis, she was slightly more approachable than her companion. But only a bit.

Her sweatshirt's fold lines were visible, like she'd stopped at a gift store nearby to make the purchase. On closer inspection, her hair looked mussed, like she'd worn a cap.

"May I help you?" Elise didn't want to commit to reopening the museum for the pair without more information. She smoothed her hair, not that she needed to. Her slicked-back bun style was her trademark, and she'd worn it so often that she'd practically trained her strands into position, fighting against flyaways.

The man shot the woman a look.

She must have taken a hint because she stepped forward, extending a hand. "Hi, I'm Kate, and this is Pete. We're in town for a few days and wanted to check out the museum. We can come back tomorrow."

Elise shook Kate's hand and shot a wary glance at Pete. Their explanation seemed slightly unnecessary. She hated the uneasy tingling along her limbs. "The museum opens at 10:00 a.m. Tours are every hour and last for about twenty minutes."

"Great, we'll be here at ten," Pete said.

His response was bright. Too bright.

If they were staying in town, they'd be at the inn and should have already known the museum hours. Unless they wanted to catch her alone. But why? She fought the shudder. Now she was letting her imagination run wild.

"I'll be here, too," Elise said with a forced smile.

The pair returned to their vehicle and drove away.

The interaction was less than a handful of minutes. But something was off. She'd worked hard to ensure the celebration year put Loon Lake on the map for all the right reasons. She shook it off and continued her inspection of the museum, picking up a discarded water bottle before heading to her car. Seth had a load of souvenirs ready for her to pick up and sell in the gift shop. She could content herself that he'd had another good day, recognized in the relative safety of their little enclave, and would shrug off her worries about the last-minute visitors.

# Chapter Two

A few hours later, Seth hummed along to the radio as he pulled a sheet of vinyl Society of Soupy stickers off the printer. This design was the most popular and his favorite. He'd worked hard to sketch the mosasaurus coming out of the water. In the murky depths below, he wrote his tagline: *the truth always surfaces.*

Inside his printshop, Print Your Way, he was nothing more than an honest, hardworking man. He had nothing to hide. He'd always been an open book to anyone who cared to read a page or a chapter. He liked living his life without secrets. He couldn't understand those who knowingly concealed or distorted facts.

He'd seen firsthand the effects of not being upfront with other people. He'd watched as secrets had clouded the formerly transparent dealings between the Inn at Loon Lake, primary employer and town benefactor, and the neighboring businesses. Thankfully, the charismatic Ashley had returned to help run the inn and doing business together became easier.

The telephone rang.

"It's a great day to Print Your Way. How may I help you?" he answered.

"Hi, honey, it's Mom."

Seth grinned at the cheerful voice on the other end. "Hey, Mom. How are you?" He glanced at the clock on the wall. "Surprised you're calling now."

"I dropped the twins off at soccer," she replied. "It's only an hour practice but at least a twenty-minute drive home, so I'm hanging out in the car."

"I'm sure Lauren appreciates you being the chauffeur," he said with a chuckle.

When Dad had died a few years earlier, Lauren, his younger sister, insisted Mom move in with her. Neither Mom nor Seth argued against the relocation. The living arrangement was almost expected. Seth had always had Dad. Mom was Lauren's go-to parent.

Lauren had graduated nursing school, gotten married, and birthed twins in rapid succession. She needed the help Mom gladly provided. Lauren's twins were every bit as athletic and sporty as their mother. Mom helped take some of the stress of running the day-to-day off Lauren.

"How's the store? How's business?" Mom asked. "Any more issues?"

"No, things are running smoothly here." For years, Mom ran the printshop alongside Dad. She had stepped down but still had advice and opinions to share.

"Because you remember last year when you couldn't get the alignment right on the menus, and you had to call—"

"I remember, Mom." He shook his head.

The bell over the door to the shop rang.

Behind the front counter, Seth had a clear view past the wall-to-wall carpeting and shelves to the glass front door and windows.

Elise strode in.

Seth's heart jumped into his throat. Like it always did. He'd spent decades in love with the beautiful, calm, composed Elise. Since the first day of kindergarten, he couldn't help but be drawn to her. She was thoughtful and careful, always knowing how to handle every situation, something he marveled at. She never made a move or said a word without consideration.

He didn't understand how that was possible. But he'd always envied her skills. When she spoke, she focused solely on one person. He loved talking with her. She made him feel like the only person in the world. He couldn't remember any of their conversations. Just the way her focus warmed him all the way through.

"Seth? Honey?" Mom asked. "Are you there?"

"Oh, sorry. Customer walked in. Talk later?" Seth asked.

"Sure thing. Bye."

He hung up the phone. "Hi, Elise," he said, too brightly, his voice chirping. He raised a fist to his mouth and coughed. "Sorry, I swallowed a bug." His cheeks burned. Why had he offered such an embarrassing excuse? He clamped his lips shut before he elaborated.

She smoothed her hair behind her ears and approached the counter. "How are you today? Did I see you out on the water earlier?"

He grinned, feeling the smile to his toes. Pulling back his shoulders, he stood ten feet tall. "Yep. I was leading a tour for Grant."

"Great weather for boating."

"Yes," he said slowly, hating to sour a pleasant conversation. But she valued honesty as much as he did. When he was with her, he'd do anything to keep her attention and earn her smiles.

He cleared his throat. "Not ideal for Soupy hunting, I'm

afraid. He prefers overcast skies and the threat of a storm. But that's okay. We had another big crowd."

She smiled back but didn't reply.

He was rambling. Again. He often lost track of his words or the point of his conversation. "Did you get a lot of visitors at the museum?"

"I had a couple," she replied slowly. A worried look crossed her features.

He frowned, wishing he could kick himself for ruining the mood with his comment. Had he forgotten to do something for the museum? Had he disappointed her somehow?

*Her event is tonight.* No wonder she was distracted. He'd finished the programs days ago and had his dress pants pressed and ready. But he forgot all about the evening's plans, and delivering her order, after he began printing stickers. The scent of ink and the warmth of the printers lulled him into a state of contentedness. "I've got your order for the kick-off celebration in the back. And the stickers for the gift shop. Everything is ready to go. I can help carry it to your car."

"Oh, right. Thanks. I forgot why I stopped in here." She chuckled and shook her head. "I guess I needed to see a friendly face."

How strange that the event had slipped her mind, too. Something like hope flared inside his chest. She wanted to see him.

"What were you doing here?" She pointed to the work-table next to the vinyl printer.

He grabbed one of the cooled stickers and held it between his fingers. "The tour boat gift shop sold out again. I haven't checked in with Zach at Scoops yet."

"It's a big year for you."

"For everyone." He hoped she was pleased with the influx of tourists his various television appearances had brought to town. Her shy smile didn't really give anything away. He pressed his tongue to the roof of his mouth. He should ask her out. Right now, before the moment passed. At least, that's what Zach would do.

Zach advised Seth on the ins and outs of romance. Although, maybe he wasn't the best choice to be a love mentor. Seth couldn't remember the last time Zach had a girl-friend or even a date. Zach never lacked for female company when he wanted it. But he kept any sort of romance casual without a repeat occurrence. Seth wanted something different. He wanted a real relationship with trust, feelings, and genuine love.

"Can I grab the order from the back?" she asked.

Seth nodded, her question taking all the air out of his puffed-out chest. "Sure, follow me." He held open the half door built into the counter and led the way into the supply room via a door in the back wall.

Rows and rows of metal shelving filled the space.

As a kid, Seth had spent his evenings and weekends in the fort he'd built out of abandoned boxes on the lowest shelf in the corner. He'd padded the shelf with cardboard and created a safe, secure cocoon. After his first encounter with Soupy, he began to sketch, write, read, and dream in the space.

He glanced at the former world headquarters for the Society of Soupy. The spot housed supplies now. While the space had changed, the store still felt like home. He might not always love the work, but he did appreciate that the business provided him with a livelihood and aided his quest. He liked carrying on Dad's work, too.

"Here we are." Seth stopped at the shelves nearest the backdoor.

One banker's box contained the pamphlets and flyers she had ordered. Another was full with merchandise for the museum gift shop. He'd given her a lot of stickers, more than she'd requested. But he believed she'd sell out. He was practicing manifestation.

He grabbed the heaviest box and opened the door, using his back to hold it. "I can help you outside."

The bell over the front door chimed.

"You'd better get that," she said. "I can make two trips."

He hated to put a customer before chivalry. "Are you sure?"

She nodded and stepped close, grabbing the box out of his arms and brushing against him in the process. "Absolutely." She exited without a glance back.

Electricity shot through him at the brief touch. He stared at his hands, expecting flames on his skin. She'd been inches away, her perfume teasing him.

"Hello?" A male voice called out.

Customers. Right. Seth stepped away from the door and raced back to the store. He'd reached the front counter again when he remembered the door was locked. He'd forgotten to prop it open. She'd have to come around through the front again. Hopefully she wouldn't be annoyed. He scrubbed a hand over his face and smiled at the customers, a man and a woman. "Hello, welcome to Print Your Way. How may I help you?"

"Are you Seth Boyd?" The man, dressed in a polo with a bright-white smile, asked.

Seth nodded. "I am."

"I'm Pete Schiller, and this is Kate Breckenridge. We're TV producers, and we've come to talk to you about Soupy," Pete said.

Seth darted his gaze from one to the other. Had he seen them on the boat earlier? He rubbed his eyes and shook his head. Maybe his eyes and ears deceived him. Was this his dream come true? He'd feared he'd missed the opportunity for a real investigation when his press started to quiet in the past few weeks.

The front door burst open.

Elise ran inside, panting. "Seth? Wait."

* * *

Elise carried the box to the car, her breathing shallow. Paper was always heavier than it looked. Inside, she'd find stacks of programs, pamphlets, and flyers. As manager of the town tourism board, she maintained a website and stocked brochures and pamphlets at the inn and other businesses along the boardwalk. Usually, she spaced out her orders to give Seth plenty of time to work and to give her plenty of reasons for stopping by.

Seth was sunshine. He always brightened her days. She'd forgotten the purpose of her visit to the printshop in light of his kind, understanding smile. He'd helped lighten her mood. One day, she'd finally ask him out.

One day. But not today. Although, she'd been very tempted to do just that. Showing up to the biggest work event of her career with a date wasn't appropriate, but she'd almost asked him to arrive with her anyway.

The second he mentioned Soupy, however, he'd raised her guard like a drawbridge over a moat. She dreaded what she knew would inevitably happen. He'd be proven wrong. His life's work reduced to a late-night punchline.

That he'd managed to escape notice from some of the more cutting comedians was a miracle unto itself. She didn't want him to take the risk of ridicule from continued exposure. And—if she was honest—nor could she.

Loon Lake had established itself as a tourist destination in the nineteenth century. A resort town that catered to families in search of recreation and the great outdoors. Miraculously, the community had stayed almost the same for over a hundred years. No major chain had ever taken up space on the board-walk. The charm of their throwback lifestyle continued to draw in guests year after year. She did not want the town to fall apart now because of Seth's vivid fantasy.

Her longtime friend might be the only person who didn't think of her as glacial. He'd always been her soft spot. She cared for him more than she'd ever admit. Because really, if she let down her guard, even for him, she worried what might happen. She liked to be in charge and prided herself on her ability to manage her emotions. Taking charge was exactly what everyone counted on her to do.

As painful as it was, she knew what she had to do right now. For Seth's sake and the town's reputation, she had to stop the Soupy sensation before the tide turned and swept them away. They'd never recover from public humiliation on a global scale.

She loaded the box into the back of her car and, after checking on the plant in the front seat, shut the door. With her time dwindling, she'd have to make a stop at the hardware store first thing in the morning. For the time being, she had to prioritize the evening event. Retreating to the back of the store, she grabbed the handle and met resistance.

The door was locked.

Of course. She'd encouraged him to rush to a customer's aid, and he'd been a little discombobulated. She didn't mind a longer walk and a wait to spend time alone. As she rounded the building and gazed across the parking lot, she stopped.

The white rental car parked at the end of the row of five businesses in front of the laundromat slash video store.

Her skin went clammy, and her body shook like she'd submerged in the lake. Her blood was ice in her veins. She hated surprises. Why couldn't she seem to avoid them lately?

"Please, please, please," she muttered as she pounded the

sidewalk under her feet and pushed open the door of the printshop with both hands. She'd had a bad feeling about the strangers. She really wanted to be wrong—though she was usually right—about her instincts.

Inside the door, however, she was once again correct.

Pete and Kate, in their khakis that were still creased from a display table, stood at the counter, chatting with Seth. No one spared her a glance.

"Seth? Wait!" she shouted.

Three heads turned in her direction.

She ignored her flaming cheeks and raced ahead, rushing behind the counter. She wasn't sure about her play here. Keep talking and insist Seth help her? Ignoring the customers? He'd be too polite to interrupt or chastise her. She could stall whatever was happening.

And then what? Follow their vehicle? She was out of her depth here. Ashley would have a plan. She wasn't as creative as her friend. In the past, she might have viewed the other woman's ideas as schemes. With the benefit of time, however, she appreciated Ashley's quick wit. But an off-the-cuff suggestion wasn't right here. The thought snapped Elise back to reality.

Elise smoothed her hair behind her ears. "Sorry, thought you were closing up. The door locked."

"Oh, right." Relief washed over Seth's features.

He really wore his heart—and every expression—on his sleeve.

"I can help in a minute. Elise, let me introduce you to Pete and Kate. They are TV producers," Seth said.

Elise clamped her lips together and shot the pair a stern look, scanning them from head to toe. Neither squirmed under her steady stare, but Pete had the sense to slip a finger under his polo collar and yank the cotton off his neck. Good.

"They want to talk about Soupy," Seth said.

Elise arched an eyebrow. Feelings had spurred her to act out of character. She'd defend Seth against any threat, including the newcomers. While their secret was revealed, they hadn't alleviated her concerns. They hadn't been transparent about their intent. She'd keep a wary watch on them. But she composed herself enough to slip back into the glacial chill of her ice queen ways.

"We want to investigate. We are looking into every angle. Every theory," Pete said.

"Your story has resonated with so many people because of the work with your dad," Kate added. "We love that. But we want to go deeper into the mystery. If there is something in the lake, we want to find it."

*NO!* Elise hated every word that came out of their mouths. The fervor had been quieting. Most of the press coverage to date had focused on the heart-tugging father-son angle. She preferred it that way.

These two people had seemed off at the museum. Their clothes and demeanors were out of place at a cabin in the middle of nowhere. Her temples throbbed with a building headache. She was missing something.

"A show will put us on the map," Seth said, stroking his chin.

He owed the town nothing. She wanted to scream at him to look out for himself first. Who cared about Loon Lake? Except, she did, and the words would ring false. She'd devoted her working life to her hometown and took pride in what she had preserved and enhanced for the entire community. Sweet Seth would be glad to help her.

"Do you have a card? A number?" Elise asked. She was tempted to remind them they'd said they'd be in town for a few days.

"Of course." Kate pulled a business card from her back pocket and slid it across the counter.

Elise stared at the fancy, embossed font, unseeing. A TV crew would draw crowds. Sure, the attention would benefit the local businesses in the short-term. But at what cost to the town in the long run? And what about Seth and his public image? "Seth, can you help me with the box?" she asked, cutting through the silence.

"We'll get going," Pete said. "Thanks for your time. Give us a call, and we can chat." He steered Kate by the shoulders toward the door.

Elise watched them leave, not moving until she was sure the door shut behind them.

"I can't believe it. This is it. The big break in the case," Seth said, sounding breathless like he'd been running.

"I don't know..."

"What else do you need to know? They want to investigate every angle. They get it. They want to shine a light on Soupy. Finally, what I've been praying for." Seth grabbed the card and kissed it, holding it to his heart. He raised his gaze to the sky. "We're getting so close, Dad."

His dad. Her heart might shatter. Mr. Boyd had been the gentlest man, and that was reflected in his son. Seth was his pride and joy. Mr. Boyd had assisted his son on every step of the journey. To invoke his memory tugged at Elise. She couldn't stand by and watch this happen. She couldn't let her friend be crushed by the world at large. If Pete and Kate were on the up and up, she didn't understand why they hadn't been forthcoming at the museum. Why the subterfuge?

"Be my manager."

"What?" She had sent some sort of mixed signal. Working with Kate and Pete was the last thing Elise wanted to do. She had enough on her plate.

"Come on. I need a John Candy."

"What?" She gasped. So much for thinking he had feelings for her.

"It's like *Cool Runnings*. No one believed Jamaica could have an Olympic bobsled team. But John Candy did. And he put them together."

She wasn't sure how a feel-good sports film had anything to do with a myth Seth invented. But at least she understood his reference and train of thought.

"People say they know they can't believe…"

She swallowed her sigh. "Jamaica's got a bobsled team." As one of the few movies available for rent throughout their childhoods at the video store and laundromat, everyone in town understood the reference.

Seth grinned. "See?"

His infectious positivity met its match today. She had too much to do to take on managing him. "For the record, John Candy didn't assemble the group. The runners teamed up and then appealed to John Candy for his expertise."

Seth held her gaze.

His enthusiasm was impossible to ignore. He melted her icy stare. She'd cave. They both knew it. Why not give in now and handle the terms that worked best for her?

"And that's what you'd be doing."

She shook her head. "I'll think about it. Help me with the last box, and I'll promise to think about it."

"That's good enough for me." Seth grinned and strode to the back of the store.

She followed reluctantly. Managing the TV crew would be a whole other job on top of her already full workload. At the minimum, they'd need to find accommodations.

The only lodging in town, the Inn at Loon Lake, sold out before the start of the summer thanks to Seth's TV appearances. Given the chance, Lonnie would upcharge the storage room over his candy store. Finding rooms was only the first and most obvious obstacle.

But she couldn't fail Seth. If she didn't take charge, she

worried she'd regret her choice. To further her goals, she'd have to manage him and the situation.

To leave a legacy, she couldn't allow any distractions. Her dreams were modest but not without their own set of challenges. As much as she loathed to admit, she could only do much on her own. While she'd like to tell Seth to forget the whole thing, she knew she couldn't. She owed him some time and consideration. Somehow she'd figure out a way for him to get what he wanted without risking her work. She didn't have a second to ponder how if she wanted to get to the kick-off celebration on time. "I'll see you tonight?"

"I wouldn't miss it," he smiled.

She wanted to stand there, smiling back at him and enjoying the warmth of his friendliness. "Great. See you in a bit." She rushed out before she could do something uncharacteristic, like kiss him.

*Chapter Three*

I nside the restored sawmill that evening, Seth scanned the polished beams that shone against rusty equipment and freshly painted walls. A display of black-and-white photographs on portable gallery walls added interest and art to the otherwise utilitarian space. The transformation was as remarkable as it was beautiful.

For years, the old sawmill had been a big, ugly box on the lakeshore. The gray siding-clad structure rose from a concrete-poured pier, hiding its history under layers of quick fixes to rotting boards. In the process, all character had been erased.

Not that Seth would ever criticize a family for doing what they could to keep their business—and home—together during challenging times. Still, he'd grown up used to the hodgepodge look. To see the transformation in the relatively short span of time, less than a year, was remarkable.

Molly had found the treasure of timbers that ultimately allowed her to stay in her family's property, rip off the seventies and eighties repairs, and restore the historic building and wheel in the lake. She used her gains for the greater good. Just like Seth hoped to.

*It's always money and time.* Dad had often spouted the wisdom whenever Seth's frustrations with not making more progress popped up. Dad's assessment had steered Seth to devote whatever of the two precious commodities he had into the project. Mostly, he'd given the search all of his free time and some of his working hours, too. He'd never regretted his choices.

Seth scanned the crowd, looking for Elise. He couldn't think her name without seeing her face in his mind. He was glad she'd agreed to help him make sense of the TV producers and their offer. While he had experience in contracts, he wasn't known for big-picture thinking. But she was.

Before the sawmill was restored to its grandeur, Lily Maguire lived in the apartment upstairs. Elise had shared with Seth that she spent a lot of time in the sawmill with Lily, helping her with simple tasks and dealing with scammers trying to trick the older lady out of her home.

"Seth? Earth to Seth? Are you in there?" Zach Jenkins, his best friend and the owner of Scoops, There It Is ice cream parlor, asked, snapping his fingers close to Seth's nose.

Seth jumped. "Hey, sorry. Didn't see you."

"I'll say." Zach grabbed a stuffed mushroom off a passing server's tray. He stuffed it in his mouth. "Why don't you just ask her out already?" He asked as he chewed.

Seth frowned. Zach knew all about Seth's longtime crush. Seth hoped he wasn't gaping at her. He didn't want everyone else to notice, too. "I don't know. She's busy."

Zach rolled his eyes and wiped his mouth with a cocktail napkin. "She's Elise. She's always busy."

"Yeah...." Seth hated to interfere with her work. He knew how important it was to her and how vital she was to everyone in town. She supported their businesses, whether they acknowledged her contributions or not.

"What about you? Any luck getting Mary to return your calls?" Seth asked, glad to turn the tables.

Mary Keith ran the dairy that supplied the cream for Scoops, There It Is. And she was the only conquest who had broken things off with Zach. She was a sore subject.

"Actually, she asked to meet at Lonnie's tomorrow afternoon."

"Oh?"

Zach grinned. "She must be coming around. She finally understands what she's missing out on."

Seth wasn't sure. But he didn't reply.

"I'm thinking of inviting her out for an early dinner and then...who knows?" Zach murmured, waggling his eyebrows.

"Good evening," Christopher Lewis, co-owner of the inn and Ashley's husband, strolled by, holding a wine glass.

Zach clamped his mouth shut. Zach hated Christopher. A lifetime of animosity between the pair had simmered under the surface of civility when they'd all been kids. As adults, however, Zach was tired of pretending.

"Hi, Christopher," Seth said, greeting the man on Zach's behalf, too. "It's a nice crowd for the kickoff, isn't it?"

Christopher nodded. "It is. The inn has been at full capacity a month earlier than usual. I owe a big thanks to you and Elise. I've had a lot of tourists return for all the events Elise planned. My guests love your tours. You and Soupy have been all the buzz at the inn."

"That's nice to hear," Seth said, feeling pleased. Christopher had no reason to seek out Seth or compliment him. Christopher's words were sincere.

"You've really put your mark on the town. You should be proud," Christopher added, sipping from his red wine.

The words held a finality, like Seth had achieved all he'd set out to do. But he was only getting started. The TV crew would shake up everything for him. He wanted to tell his friends about the visitors he'd had today.

But he wasn't sure Elise would approve. He needed her on board. He darted a glance at Elise again, now in conversation with Molly and Ashley. Working with Elise on the project would be a great excuse to get close to her and maybe ask her out.

"I'm sure she's thrilled, too," Christopher said.

Seth darted his gaze between his friends. He was being too obvious. "Tonight is her success. We should celebrate her."

"You could ask her out..." Zach said.

"Right now? Seriously?" Christopher asked.

Zach waggled his eyebrows.

"Zach is giving you dating advice? Based on what experience?" Christopher scoffed.

Zach narrowed his gaze, glowering at the other man.

Seth appreciated both men for their strengths, namely their respective approaches to self-confidence, and looked past any failings. He considered Zach and Christopher friends and counted on their support for his efforts, both with Soupy and the store. The inn was the biggest client. But Zach stocked stickers and coasters for the monster hunt. Together, they worked on *Loon Lake Life*. Seth held out hope that the two men would eventually realize they had more in common and forge a friendship, or even a friendly acquaintance, but was okay with a thaw of their glacial hatred for one another.

Laughing at each other wasn't the right approach.

"I have dated more than one woman, you know," Zach said. "Not everyone marries their childhood sweetheart before finishing their undergrad degree."

Seth cringed, bracing himself. Zach might reveal his numerous flings over the years with Christopher's guests to prove himself. Zach loved to rankle Christopher. In response, with his hackles raised, Christopher would retort with something curt and cutting. Then the bickering would start, and they'd cause another scene. But this time, they'd ruin Elise's night. The same old patterns no longer worked.

While Seth had no interest in one-night stands, he couldn't deny Zach had plenty of experience chatting up women. The only few who seemed immune to his charms were Molly, Ashley, and Elise.

*Don't say anything.*

"Maybe I'd better steer clear of this conversation. I'd hate to interfere with a love guru," Christopher said, sarcasm dripping off his every word and his jaw twitched.

*"If you listened to Zach Jenkins 50 percent less, you'd be 150 percent better off."*

Mom's words filtered through Seth's mind. Despite the miles between them, his mom remained a prominent figure in his life. He'd absorbed so much of her advice over the years that he imagined what she would say like his very own cricket conscience, sitting on his shoulder.

"Good evening," Grant interrupted, striding into the group with a broad grin, seemingly oblivious to the heated atmosphere. "What did I miss?"

"Nothing," Seth blurted. "Actually, I'm glad you are here. I had an idea for all three of you."

"Oh?" Grant asked.

Seth nodded, ignoring Zach's tense jaw and Christopher's narrowed gaze, the each man ready to attack the other. "Yes, yes, of course," Seth stalled. "A map. Like a treasure map."

Christopher gaped.

Grant shuddered.

Zach raised both eyebrows.

Until Seth had said the words out loud, he hadn't anticipated the poor reception. Although he should have. Treasure was a sore topic after the pursuit of riches had threatened the lives of three Loon Lake residents over two different incidents a year earlier. "Not like that. No shovels. No gold," Seth added. "I was thinking of something for kids to do on the hunt for Soupy. Stop at points along the lakeshore to observe the water. Earn stickers for turning in their findings at each stop. You never know. Kids are smart and clever. I wouldn't mind if someone else found a lead."

And then Seth could share that with the camera crew. If he signed the contract... he gave himself a shake. He'd wait for Elise's answer. It wouldn't work without her help. He knew that in his bones.

"I don't know," Grant murmured. "I nearly died on the last treasure hunt. I'm not eager to join another."

"Maybe next year," Christopher replied. "Not to put you off. But I think it's a little too soon after everything that happened with the Prims."

Grant opened his mouth and quickly shut it.

"Is there something else?" Seth prodded.

"No, no. I have no facts to share," Grant replied with a shaky smile.

But he knew something. A gut feeling? Seth valued instincts and always trusted his.

"Why wait?" Zach asked with his usual confident swagger, clapping a hand on Seth's shoulder. "I'll support you. Whatever you want to do to get answers, you have me. Always."

Christopher rolled his eyes. "This isn't about not being supportive. I hope you've always felt encouraged by the inn and our programs. It's just that—"

"You are living in the past," Zach interrupted. "You're afraid to move forward."

The only way to diffuse the never-ending argument between Zach and Christopher was to walk away. "You know you're both right. It is too soon for the map. And Zach, if you'll excuse me? I'll take your advice."

Shaking out of Zach's hold, Seth strode away before either

could stop him with another word. A lot of times, he acted without much thought. Maybe the problem was that he spent too much time in his head when it came to Elise. If he wanted a different result, he needed to change the action.

* * *

Elise scanned the old sawmill, taking in the scene. She'd found a spot near one of the original support beams to observe and catch her breath. The space was packed. The admission fee hadn't discouraged curious locals from stopping by to spy Molly's handiwork. With any luck, the money raised tonight would be a solid start for the foundation.

All Elise had to do was keep up the high level of quality with the rest of her civic celebrations so that when she sent requests for year-end donations, she'd receive support. And she probably had to socialize and make small talk. Networking was part of fundraising, too. She stepped away from the beam, making a slight effort to look approachable.

Servers carried trays of hors d'oeuvres and bottles of wine, refilling guests' glasses. The large, open space of the mill had been somewhat divided up with movable walls, showcasing Molly's photography.

If Elise had had her way, accepting the museum on behalf of the town and taking it over as the official historical society headquarters, she would not have been able to move half as fast in the restoration of the building. *A Maguire in possession of the mill is prosperity for all.* Like many things in their tight-knit community, the words became legend and—for a while—a self-fulfilling prophecy.

What Molly had achieved was remarkable. Elise admitted the truth. While the pair had a rough start, they had moved past their animosity to mutual respect. Not necessarily friend-ship, but Elise didn't need confidantes. She was content to keep her own counsel, much the way she would never fall in love. Other people were too much of an unknown factor for her equilibrium. She might have flirted with the idea of pursuing something more with Seth. But she couldn't cross the line.

She wouldn't endanger a friendship for what would probably be a lackluster kiss. She couldn't risk losing the one person that really mattered because she spent too much time thinking about making out with him or pondering how firm his biceps were under his t-shirts.

"You certainly delivered a crowd," Molly said, striding toward her arm in arm with Ashley.

Elise shook her head. "The sawmill is remarkable. You drew the crowd. Thank you for hosting this evening. I'm sure this first launch will be a big success."

"I'm happy to do my part. I know my arrival threw a wrench in your plans. Glad to see I was only a momentary setback," Molly replied.

"I agree this event is wonderful. You both have done a marvelous job," Ashley chimed in, waving to a server. "We should toast."

The server approached, and each woman grabbed a champagne flute.

"To a spectacular start and a mutually beneficial arrangement," Ashley said, raising her glass. "We know the inn's catering is up to snuff now. I look forward to expanding our business."

Molly giggled. "Just keep that in mind as I open the building for events."

"I'm counting on it," Ashley replied with a wink.

The silly exchange was typical of their friendship. The women stood arm in arm. Elise was again on the outside. In the past, Ashley wouldn't have included her in the conversation at all. Elise would have to accept the slow thawing between them and stop trying to read into every comment.

But Elise didn't do silly. She spoke with purpose and didn't waste her energy on entertaining others. She wasn't a performer.

She raised her glass to the other two and clinked. "Cheers." She brought her champagne close to her lips but didn't drink. Alcohol was another one of those uncontrollable elements she steered away from. She kept a level head always.

"Well, your planning is flawless as always," Ashley said. "Let me know what else you need from the inn to assist with the other special events."

"Oh, I can't wait for the parade," Molly chimed in. "I've bought tons of candy. I had to store it at the boathouse so I'd stop snacking."

"We should be good until the final meeting for the fun run, although..." Elise nibbled her lip. Did she share Seth's news? What would the women think? She'd never had the urge to get someone else's take on a situation before. She was completely discombobulated by the day.

Ashley stared at her expectantly.

They'd known each other since childhood, and while never close, they knew the other well enough to sense something unspoken and important.

"Are you worried about the Soupy Seekers?" Molly asked, sipping her wine and completely unaware of the change of tone.

"Soupy Seekers?" Ashley asked, grinning. "What a marvelous name. You have to share that with Seth."

Molly laughed, her chortle enhanced and loosened by the drink.

Were they laughing at Seth or with him? Elise couldn't tell. She was never sure how the townsfolk interpreted Seth. Lovable or laughable? She hoped for the former. Because he was not a joke, and she wouldn't let him become anyone's punchline.

"Good evening, everyone," a deep voice said over a microphone. "Shall we ask our event organizer to say a few words?"

Elise turned toward the center of the room, spotting Lonnie from the taffy store at the mic. If she wasn't being looked at, she would have rolled her eyes. Lonnie loved a little attention.

"Why isn't Tim introducing you?" Ashley said with a frown. "He's the mayor."

"Is Lonnie mad he lost the election to Tim?" Molly offered.

Having only been in town for a year, Molly already understood the dynamics of long-running feuds in the community. Animosity simmered under the surface. Elise would do well to nip whatever display of ego was happening in the bud. "If you'll excuse me," Elise said, backing away from the pair and crossing toward Lonnie. While she wasn't prepared for a speech, she was glad to break away from Molly and Ashley. Elise was running out of small talk.

She offered Lonnie a tight smile. Before the campaign, she wouldn't have pegged Lonnie as a public speaker.

Bending low, Lonnie bowed and stepped to the side, offering her the center stage spot.

Did the crowd wonder if her icy exterior would melt under the hot lights? At least her stoic reputation meant she didn't have to waste time or energy smiling. "Thank you for that introduction and for putting me on the spot."

A few pained chuckles sounded from the crowd.

"I really don't have a speech prepared. I'll try not to ramble and keep this brief. First, a huge thank you to both Molly Maguire and the Lewises for hosting and catering this event." Elise clapped.

Molly waved, and Ashley made a grand, over-the-top bow.

A whistle sounded from the back.

"Now, now. This isn't a bachelorette auction," Elise said. "We are here for the first-ever fundraiser for the Loon Lake Historical Museum and Society. Everyone here is a local. You all know how special this town is and, over the past year, I think we have all come to appreciate how important our stories are. We are more than a spot on a map. We are a community. An interconnected network of people that includes both generational legacies and brand-new transplants. But we all choose to be here. Our town has endured a lot over the last twelve months."

She paused for the murmurs she knew that comment would elicit.

Her gaze darted through the crowd, gauging the reactions and noting Grant's solemn expression and Christopher's stoic frown. Those two had certainly dealt with their fair share of the drama caused by the Prims. But with the father and son behind bars, and their dastardly lawyer apprehended too, no one had anything to fear. Except for her.

"And I, personally, have come to understand more than ever how nothing is guaranteed in this life. If something is important, it needs attention and care. To that end, I'm determined to make sure the historical museum and society are fully funded for the future and will continue beyond my tenure. This fabulous event has raised over five figures, which is a very nice start. But this is just the beginning. As the town celebrations continue with the fun run and the parade, I hope we will raise three times that amount by the end of the year before the town budget meeting in January."

"Me too," a male voice called out in the crowd.

The guests parted as Mayor Tim Burt strode forward. "I'm happy to leave you in charge and take all the credit."

The crowd laughed.

So did Elise, although she hated the public display of self-deprecation. Tim wasn't a micromanager and left her to her own devices, just as his father had before him. He respected her and her hard work. If something went wrong, she hoped to count on Tim's support.

With her renewed focus, she had no reason to fear testing out the depths of Tim's loyalty. If she helped Seth, she risked making a mess of her life—personally and professionally. Or she could take charge with her trademark icy steel grip. "Thank you for your generosity this evening and for your town loyalty. Our stories matter, and thank you all for trusting me to preserve our part in the town's long history. I'll make you proud." She nodded at Tim. "I'll do my best for all of you. Please enjoy your evening."

Applause sounded.

Heat flamed Elise's cheeks. She hated being the focus of any attention and gladly stepped to the side. But she did want transparency. While she had no official boss, she considered every member of town to be her employer. She hoped she'd make everyone proud. And, if she messed up, she'd be reprimanded by Tim, or so her self-doubt assured her.

A server approached with a tray of champagne, separating her from the mayor. She grabbed another glass, needing something for both hands to hold so she didn't twist her fingers together and display her nerves to the world.

Turning, she took a few steps and collided with a man, spilling a little champagne. "Oh, Seth. Hi, sorry. Did I splash you?"

He stared down at his dark gray pants and tucked in dress shirt. "Nope. I'm fine. You look very nice."

She wore her little black dress, a cap-sleeve and mid-calf-length slightly form-fitting frock she'd had forever. The outfit was practically a uniform, her go-to for any dressy event. But no one had ever complimented her on it before. "Thanks."

She extended the mostly full glass. "Here. It's the least I can do."

He waved her off and grabbed another from a passing server. "I liked your speech. You're right. Preserving our stories is important. I've learned that over the past year, too."

She sipped from her glass, the bubbles tickling the roof of her mouth as she swallowed. "Thanks. It's a big year for the town and a lot to manage on top of my other duties. But it's too important a time to let any opportunity slip by."

In a town full of big personalities, Elise had made it her mission to preserve everyone's story. Ashley, Christopher, Grant, Molly, and even Zach would be immortalized in town history without any help from her. What about the rest of them? Like Seth? The documentary was a huge opportunity and platform to add Seth's story to that history.

"I don't want to make assumptions anymore. I don't want to be caught by surprise," Elise cleared her throat.

"Have you had a chance to think about being my manager? I really don't think this is a chance I can miss."

She nodded, pursing her lips. She knew he'd say that and feel it, too. Perhaps the TV documentary was the only way to dissuade him from his outlandish theory. He would be crushed.

She couldn't take on one more thing. But neither could she leave him to his own devices. He needed coverage.

If she didn't shield him, she feared he'd turn to Zach next. No Tact Zach would cause chaos. She definitely didn't have time to clean up whatever mess he left behind. Besides, being in charge of Seth's image would help her reassert control over her own feelings. She'd realign herself with him in a professional capacity. She couldn't let emotions compel her to act with her heart. She'd choose her head. "I have."

"And?"

"What if you don't like the answers you learn?"

"I'm not afraid of being wrong. I'm more scared of never taking a chance."

His words hit her in the stomach like a punch. As much as she might want to, she couldn't argue with his bravery. She drained her glass and handed it to a passing server. She stuck out her hand. "I'll manage you. I'll call Kate and Pete and let them know we can meet at your store tomorrow afternoon."

"Really? Oh you won't regret this."

She rather suspected she would.

He lifted an arm, like he'd pull her in for a side hug.

She froze, and shock must have flashed in her gaze because he lowered his arm quickly and extended a fist instead.

The light tap to her inner elbow barely registered as a touch. The awkward moment was another missed connection. But she shivered at the contact and plastered on a smile. What she wouldn't do was forget the sheer spark of joy flashing in his eyes. She had done that. She had created that little burst of happiness for him. She wished it would be enough.

*Chapter Four*

Seth never drank coffee. The bitter flavor bothered his tongue, and he found the mere aroma overwhelming. But right now, the morning after the sesquicentennial kickoff gala, he wished he had a strong cup of caffeine both to jolt him to full awareness and to use as a prop as he darted his attention between Zach and Christopher like he watched a high-powered tennis match. His neck hurt from the constant swiveling. His head pounded from the verbal volleying.

Both men were too sharp and too quick to gain ground at the expense of the other. When Seth had made plans with Zach to review the latest issue of *Loon Lake Life* before printing, Seth had written the date and time on a sticky note on the counter. Later that same day, when Christopher had asked to meet to discuss the new menus for the inn, Seth had repeated the hour and day that popped into his head.

Beyond the typical catty comments, Seth's exhaustion was entirely his fault. He had stayed awake too late after coming home from the sawmill, unable to sleep for the excitement of what lay ahead. Elise had agreed to manage him. The TV producers were stopping by in a little bit to sign contracts. He was thrilled but also apprehensive.

He hadn't had a chance to discuss the news with Mom and Lauren, he'd missed calling them in the short window before work and the school drop-off. He didn't need their advice, and he knew they wouldn't discourage him. But he hated not informing them before something happened. Their family didn't keep secrets.

Later, he vowed, he'd find time to call and explain everything. Now, he was exhausted. He covered his mouth with a hand and yawned.

"See? Everyone is tired of your childish behavior," Christopher crowed over Zach, crossing his arms. "If you won't back off for my sake or Ashley's, why not for Elise? She's worked too hard to have her events overshadowed by your slander."

Oh no. Seth needed to focus. His mind wandered to other things while his body remained present for what was becoming another full-blown battle.

Zach rolled his eyes. "I am not attacking Ashley or Elise. I'm merely pointing out that one person's continued property monopoly in the community puts everyone at risk. And Seth is exhausted with you, not me."

Seth opened his mouth to jump in and yawned again.

"Seriously, are you okay?" Zach asked. "You look rough."

"Maybe your blinding white overalls and neon shirt are a little too much to look at first thing in the morning," Christopher quipped, adjusting his necktie and smoothing his dress shirt into pressed chinos.

Each man showed up in their work uniforms, a visual disparity further highlighting their differences.

Seth scrubbed a hand over his face. If he rubbed hard enough, he could erase whatever expression he wore. "I have a lot on my mind today. Sorry I double-booked you two."

"What's going on? Do you need more love advice?" Zach asked. He stuck out his chest and lifted his chin.

As usual, Zach exuded confidence. His meeting with Mary was hours away, but that didn't seem to concern him at all. Seth wondered how his friend found such certainty in himself when all signs pointed to another romantic dead end.

Christopher snorted.

"No, not that," Seth said. "And maybe I'm wrong to trust my instincts." He spoke from his heart.

"Always trust your instincts," Christopher said soberly, wiping a hand over his chin. "I should drop my petty behavior with Zach. We called a truce. We need to honor it." He extended a hand to his nemesis.

"Fine." Zach sighed. "You're right. But I'm not shaking on it. I won't engage in your *bigger-person antics* and give you the credit for suggesting a treaty." He tucked his hands under his armpits.

Seth twitched his nose, making a note not to shake his friend's hand. He glanced at germ-conscious Christopher and spotted the upper lip curling in disgust.

"What do you mean about trusting your gut?" Zach asked.

Seth wasn't sure he should say. He didn't want to jinx anything before the TV producers officially offered him a contract. Elise would remain calm and collected. She would wait until everything was legal and settled. And he should do the same.

"Seth? What's going on?" Christopher asked, peering at him.

Seth darted his gaze to the door, but no one walked by. It was still too early for tourists to drop in. Mostly, he met business clients in the mornings at their locations. He didn't have to worry about anyone interrupting him for a scheduled appointment. But he hoped Elise might come in and take charge like she did so well. "I'm getting a TV show about Soupy."

Christopher stared, slack-jawed.

"For real? For really real?" Zach stammered. "Like, for really, really real?"

"I haven't signed the contracts yet. That's happening in a little bit. But yes, for real," Seth said.

"How?" Christopher asked. "I mean. Did you seek them out? Call up a production company? Search the internet?"

Seth shook his head. "Nope. They came to me yesterday. But I looked them up, and they are legit." He paused, waiting for nineties-loving Zach to make a "too legit to quit." joke. But when the silence merely stretched, Seth wasn't sure what to make of it.

Dumbfounded by his luck or skeptical about his chance for success? He'd handled his fair share of critics over the years. But he had never heard a negative word from this pair.

"What does your mom think?" Zach asked.

"I haven't told her. Nothing is official yet." Seth shrugged, his shaggy hair bobbing with the movement. "I know she'll support me." His sister would be the difficult one to convince. "I guess it doesn't feel real. Talking about it is...strange."

"Do you need any help? Any assistance?" Christopher asked, running a hand through his short hair.

"Elise is helping," Seth said.

The pair nodded in unison.

Seth was glad to have earned approval without question. In a town full of legacies, it was hard to stand out and set oneself apart. He was glad for the chance to cement his and Dad's significance in the town's history. He'd grown so used to being a sidekick and had never had hope for real progress on finding Soupy.

Now, with official backing, he had to deliver. He'd been chasing the opportunity his whole life, and he couldn't fail.

"We'll help in any way we can," Christopher said.

"Absolutely." Zach chimed in. "I'm always ready for my close-up."

"We all want *you* to succeed," Christopher added and shot Zach a hard look.

"Of course, we do. But a little TV coverage won't hurt any of us," Zach replied.

Seth nodded. He was glad for their readiness to join in the filming. The community's support meant the world to Seth. Without his friends' and neighbors' backing, he wouldn't have hit publish on his memoir. "We haven't discussed any specifics, yet," Seth said. "They want to do a full investigation of the lake. They said every method will be utilized to hunt for Soupy. I don't know about interviews. But I'll give them your names. I'm sure they'll be in touch."

"Ashley and Mr. Willie, too," Christopher said. "No one knows the terrain like Mr. Willie. And Ashley's always wanted to appear on camera."

Seth nodded. Ashley was so magnetic He wanted her blessing, however he could get it. Mr. Willie, the longtime groundskeeper at the inn, was an expert on the local landscape. The inn owned the largest stretch of lakeshore property. Kate and Pete would want to talk to the leading expert about the topography.

"And Grant and Molly," Zach said. "Grant especially will be able to help with access to the lake. They might be newcomers, but they had that incident on the open water last summer."

Seth reached for a stack of sticky notes and jotted down the names. Firsthand accounts would be especially important for any investigation. "Good ideas. If you get more, tell me."

The bell over the front door chimed.

"Elise is here," Zach murmured.

Seth glanced up and grinned as Elise neared.

"Best behavior," Christopher said, shooting Zach a look.

Zach rolled his eyes. "When am I not my best?"

Christopher opened his mouth to reply but thought better of it.

Elise stepped up to the counter. Her eyes darted side to side, taking in his companions. "Good morning. Am I too early? I don't want to interrupt your business."

Her tone was professional and distant. Her hesitation gave Seth pause. He hoped she was on edge because of the ongoing cold war between Zach and Christopher. Their verbal assaults rarely ceased. Walking in on one of their disagreements was a lot to deal with for a morning after a major event.

Seth hoped so, at least. He didn't want her to have second thoughts about managing him. He wanted more time together. "Right on time. We were just finishing up."

"Exciting news about the documentary crew. Let us know whatever you need," Christopher said.

Elise pressed her lips together and tipped her head to the side.

Sometimes, the tiny acknowledgement was all the confirmation Elise would display. Seth knew the quiet and small gestures could be as emphatic as one of Zach's exuberant agreements.

"I better get set up at the ice cream shop; good to see you both," Zach said.

"I'll walk out with you," Christopher said, nodding at Seth and Elise. "Good luck."

Seth waved. He didn't need luck. With Elise and Soupy, he had everything he could ever need. He was winning.

* * *

Elise would have preferred to sign the contracts before Seth shared his news with the two biggest gossips in town. As Zach and Christopher retreated, however, she contented herself with a few minutes to get her thoughts—and their plan—in order. They would need to be a team to make this work, not simply following the whims of Kate and Pete.

Pulling back her shoulders and tugging the hem of her blazer, she steadied herself before turning to him.

"I probably shouldn't have said anything to Zach and Christopher," Seth said slowly, his brow knitting together. "I am so excited I can't contain myself."

She released the breath she'd been holding and loosened a bit of the steel from her spine. She was dealing with Seth. Lovable, good-hearted, handsome Seth. She'd have to make allowances for his unbridled joy. It was one of the qualities she loved about him.

*Loved?*

"It's okay. But I want us to get on the same page about..." She pointed her finger between the two of them and then circled her wrist to include the store. "We have a lot at play. Before we sign any contracts or discuss any deals, we need to understand each other. I want to support you and your vision. But what do you want out of this arrangement? What does getting a TV deal mean? How many episodes are you agreeing to? Will this be a series? A one-time special? Do you want to license the program to streaming services or stick to network TV?" Until she started talking, she hadn't really thought about all the options either. She overwhelmed herself.

He stroked his chin. "I hadn't really put too much thought into the details. I want to find Soupy. I want to get to the truth."

She nodded. "How do you feel about the townspeople being interviewed and included? They'll want more than just you on camera." But he was the heart.

"I'll be glad for it. Especially if they can get Mr. Willie on the record. I know he's seen something," Seth said.

Mr. Willie had more firsthand knowledge of the inn's portion of the lake than any other person alive or dead. "Have you asked him about Soupy before?"

"I have, and he doesn't respond. He walks away, every time."

The tidbit was interesting and a fact to file away for another time. "Well, don't let the whole project devolve into everyone else's fifteen minutes of fame. I'll discuss an interview list with the TV team and might have pre-meetings with our neighbors." She would do anything she could to control the narrative. The community's best interests guided her every action.

Seth's Soupy mania was in direct odds with her organized, efficient tourism. The documentary crew added a whole other headache, threatening to make a mockery of everyone. Soupy wasn't real. Would it be better for her to break the news to him or let him find out on camera?

Her motivation had nothing to do with romantic feelings, and everything to do with preserving the town for the next hundred-plus years. She almost convinced herself of the lie. Maybe she was a coward, not admitting her feelings.

"Okay," she said, smiling at him even though she didn't feel the grin in her bones. "I get it. I'm on board. Now let's get some answers."

The front door opened, the bell chiming.

Right on time. Whether or not she was a skeptic or a believer, she couldn't deny her intuition.

Dressed in windbreakers and chinos, Kate and Pete looked like they were trying to blend in with their surroundings in the blandest way possible. Maybe this sort of corporate casual worked as camouflage in the rest of the world, but in Loon Lake, where everyone stood out—from Zach in his bright fluorescents and white overalls at his ice cream shop to Ashley in her flowy dresses—the pair were conspicuous.

"Good morning," Kate greeted, extending a hand to first Elise and then Seth. "Thanks for the phone call and meeting with us today. We're really looking forward to working together to discover the secrets of Loon Lake."

"Good morning," Seth said. "Nice to see you again."

Elise simply tilted her head. She preferred to let others do most of the talking. She was an active listener.

"Right, so," Pete said, coughing into his fist. "We didn't officially meet yesterday. Kate is a director and producer, mostly working on documentaries. I'm a host and producer. We have never worked in the cryptid field before, but we are very eager to dive into the jaws, so to speak." He forced a laugh.

"What we are proposing is that we conduct several searches of the lake. We'd like to use sonar, DNA, that sort of thing," Kate said, her expression serious.

Pete had sobered up, too. Good. He must have caught on that humor and jesting about Seth's passion wasn't going to earn him any points here. While Pete might be charming in another place, he was almost boorish here.

"What do you mean by DNA?" Seth asked. "Are you proposing a cheek swab or something?"

Pete chuckled.

"While that's a very interesting thought," Kate said. "New research takes samples of the lake and is so sensitive that it can analyze the DNA of every living thing in the water. If a dog has jumped into the water, it'll show up. The results are astounding."

Elise nibbled her cheek. How did scientists identify DNA from an extinct species? From fossilized mosquitoes in amber?

"And we'd like to do interviews as well," Pete added. "Seth, you, of course, will be on camera for most of our shots. We'd like you to be actively participating in the scientific searches of the lake. You are our star."

Elise wanted assurances that Seth would remain the focus. With a lifetime of experiences, she worried about the involvement of the other egos in town. She and Seth weren't the flashy, front-and-center people in their community. But that didn't mean their stories weren't just as valid. Memorializing every family and their role in town was her goal with the historical society. "How long will you be here?" Elise asked. And how much would they impact her celebration year? "How many people will you be bringing?"

"I'm anticipating several months," Kate said. "And we'll keep the crew small to save expenses and not draw too much attention to ourselves. We don't really want crowds."

Kate was clearly the lead, and she seemed savvy enough to understand Elise was the boss. Elise could come to respect the other woman even if her first impression was of a person skulking around. Elise had been right then, and she knew she was correct now. "Seth's already made a name for himself. Our town's bookings are up this summer. Finding lodging might be difficult, and keeping crowds away will be almost impossible."

Elise glanced at Seth, the man vibrating from either excitement or nerves. She hadn't seen him like this since high school when they'd waited together to find out if he passed the science test so he could graduate on time. She'd helped him with tutoring back then. She'd do what she could for him now. "Okay, let's look at the contracts."

If Elise prided herself on one personality trait, it was her ability to stay unflappable no matter what was happening around her.

As she read every word of the contracts, she tuned out the individual voices nearby. Kate, Pete, and Seth's voices became indistinguishable tones. The white noise didn't speed up Elise's reading or slow her down. She continued at her own pace, making notes in a notebook she kept in her purse for such occasions.

She wasn't in the habit of signing binding legal documents every day. But she'd had to jot down something important at least once a day for the past several years, since taking over the tourism board. Of course, she'd never written details concerning the use of name, image, and likeness before.

That was the section of the contract that made her uncomfortable. The language was not vague. Only Seth was covered by the indemnification clause, agreeing to cover any unforeseen costs arising from his involvement, and not the town at large. She knew he'd agree to it in a second. He was eager to appear on TV and get more attention on his search.

She had never had any desire for fame, and that was the very same few sentences that would have decided her against the whole endeavor. The words publish, advertise, announce, and use in any manner or medium in connection with any exercise by licensee were transcribed and circled. "Seth, please come here and read this," she said, stopping at the counter and tapping a finger to the spot.

He leaned down, lowering his lanky frame to peer over her shoulder. His breath tickled her neck. He smelled like hot ink on paper and fresh laundry, an intoxicating combination.

She swallowed. She should have handed him the pages and not set herself up for his distracting nearness.

"Well?" Kate asked.

Seth pulled back. "I'm okay with that," he said, lightly squeezing Elise's shoulder.

Elise fought to keep her reaction neutral. She worried he didn't understand every implication inherent in the legalese. Her concern for his portrayal wasn't alleviated by what she read. But she couldn't fight him at every turn, or he'd stop asking for her advice.

"Then you are good to sign," Elise said.

He fist pumped the air. "I know this is the right choice."

"Me too," Pete added.

Kate handed Seth a pen.

He signed the last page with a flourish and slid the contract to Kate. "What now?"

Kate stuffed the contract into her purse. "We return to LA and get our crew assembled. We'll be back in a couple weeks with equipment for filming and for the investigation. You just get yourself ready. Find old notes, old photographs, any and every piece of documentation you've put together over the years. We'll need it all," Kate said.

"What about call sheets? Craft services? Reviewing a list of shots? Coordinating interviews? Signing off permission to appear on camera?" Elise asked.

"Someone's done their research," Kate replied.

Elise couldn't read the tone. Snarky? Supportive? The words held a hint of something under the polite veneer. "Yes, I like to be prepared."

"If you could help us with waivers for the 5k? Did we read that correctly on your blog? Or was it a webpage?" Kate asked.

The last word was clunky. Sure, Elise didn't have exceptional technical skills and couldn't code. But the town's website was up to date and easy to navigate. "Of course I can handle that for you. Should we print those off now?"

"Plenty of time for figuring out all of that later. I really admire your zest for getting the job done. First, we should celebrate," Pete said. "Can we take you out for a drink? Maybe at the inn?"

"Yes, I'm in," Seth said.

*And I should warn Tim.* She hadn't had a chance to touch base with the mayor about the interesting opportunity for Seth. Since the joking callout at the kick-off event, she hadn't spared Tim a thought. He needed to be aware of anything impacting the town.

"Can you join us, Elise?" Kate asked.

"Please go ahead without me. I need to run an errand," Elise replied.

Seth shot her a confused, dazed look.

"Really. Go and have a nice toast to Soupy. I have to do something." Elise swung her purse over her arm and swiftly exited the printshop.

She made her way down the row of stores in the strip mall until she reached the very end. Burt's Hardware and More had been the main livelihood supporting the family of civil servants since the town's founding. The Burts supplied both the material needs and the civic wants of Loon Lake.

Elise entered the store, a bell ringing overhead as she pushed through the entryway.

"Good afternoon, how may I help you today?" Tim called from behind the front counter.

Elise darted her gaze through the interior.

"Just me at the moment, I'm afraid," Tim said.

She approached the front counter. "Nothing scary in that. I was hoping to speak with you."

"Of course. Is this official town business?" Tim asked. "Because I wanted to clarify my comments. I was only teasing. You know you can count on me for whatever you need. I would never take credit for your success." He chuckled. "Not that anyone would let me."

She smiled at that, both at his accurate assessment and his return to self-effacement. Tim had taken on a grander attitude during the campaign to replace his father. She was glad for the good guy she'd known her whole life and the return of his down-to-earth personality. "Thanks, Tim. I appreciate that. I actually have news to share on behalf of Seth Boyd. But it will sort of concern you, and I wanted you to be aware."

Tim folded his arms over his chest. "I'm all ears."

"A documentary crew will be filming Seth and helping him with a scientific investigation of the lake."

"The search for Soupy gets syndicated? Soup's on."

She swallowed her groan at both his terrible pun and the implication he hinted at. How terrible to catch reruns for the rest of her life of this moment in time. How would she explain it to her grandkids? Maybe that was getting ahead of herself. She'd need kids first and a serious boyfriend before that. But still, the idea that she might turn on a television and unwittingly catch a glimpse of herself in the background from this very summer was sort of unnerving.

"I think that's great. Seth wants answers. Hopefully, this will give him some. And you must be pleased," Tim said.

She must? Why? She knit her brows together, feeling the scrunch from the inside of her head.

"More attention will mean more visitors. You're already doing a bang-up job. This will just put you over the top. Maybe get you more sign-ups for the fun run, too."

She kept her expression neutral, fighting the urge to frown or gape at the mention of the 5k. Kate and Pete hadn't answered her most pertinent questions and instead distracted her with the race. Elise didn't love another mention and wasn't a big believer in coincidence.

"Every little bit counts for the foundation, right?" Tim prodded.

"Yes, exactly. You're perfectly correct." She vowed to look at it from that perspective and stop seeing conspiracy or manipulation. The fun run was happening soon. Ticket sales weren't quite what she'd hoped. If word got out about a camera crew, how many wannabe celebrities might descend on the town to try to get into shots? "The production will include the race."

"Wonderful news. I will help you in any way you need, and I'll spread the word about filming. You're not alone. Just give me a heads-up, okay?" Tim asked. "I want to be involved and assist you."

"Absolutely. Thanks. I'll keep you posted." With a wave, she left the store and headed straight to her car. She'd leave the schmoozing at the inn to Seth and go home to focus on her own work. She'd have a little bit of a break before the cameras started rolling. And then?

She wasn't sure what would happen. But she'd find a way to keep it all contained. She wouldn't need Tim's help or anyone's. She never had. And she never would.

*Chapter Five*

Two weeks had passed since signing the contract. Had Seth dreamed the interest in the search for Soupy? Kate and Pete had departed straight away with promises to return as soon as they gathered their crew.

While fourteen days wasn't a particularly long time to wait, each second stretched to an hour. Seth had kept to his routine, leading sold-out tours and running the printshop. He had spoken with Elise a few times, but she hadn't had any updates about filming either.

Instead, she had focused on her work and told him to do the same. Luckily, the Soupy fun run was approaching soon, giving him plenty of opportunity to see her. He'd had an idea to make a special, limited-edition sticker, modifying his popular Society of Soupy design, for all participants.

His efforts weren't entirely selfless. He wanted another excuse for her to stop by and chat. Filming would bring them together, but until it commenced, he found himself alone and at loose ends. The longer he waited for filming, the more he became convinced it wouldn't happen. Too good to be true haunted him. So he tried to find other things to keep him busy.

Elise probably had no such trouble. Besides her upcoming events, she had logistics to handle for the crew. She had been coordinating accommodations for them at the inn. He'd offered his help several times, but she'd politely declined.

The bell over the printshop's front door chimed.

"Good morning," Elise greeted, her smile bright and her steps light.

Seth was always happy for a chance to see her. But she had a breeziness today. "Hi, how are you?"

"I'm great." She stopped at the counter. "Did you get my text?"

He frowned. "Text?" Patting his pockets and surveying the counter, he didn't see his phone.

"Well, maybe it's better to catch you off guard," she said, slightly breathless. "The crew arrived and is heading over."

Seth widened his gaze and pointed at the ground. "Here, as in, here? Now?" His palms went clammy, and he dried them against his jeans. He'd been so anxious for the project to start, but he hadn't really thought it would.

"Yes, now. The inn was fully booked for the summer. Ashley and Christopher have graciously agreed to move out of their marital home and into a studio apartment attached to the office on the inn's top floor, to make plenty of room for the crew. It's been a major headache," she said.

With each word, Seth gripped the edge of the counter a little tighter, holding himself in reality so he didn't drift away.

"I texted as soon as I had word they'd arrived. It's been chaotic. Are you feeling alright?" She pressed a cool palm to his forehead.

He stopped himself from leaning into her touch. "I'll be fine."

She dropped her hand. "We can still back out."

He shook his head. They couldn't. Besides the hefty fee he'd owe, he needed to take this step. He had to get proof of Soupy's existence and seal his place in the town's history. "I can do this. Did you know they planned to start today? Do you have a schedule?"

"They handed me a timeline a little bit ago, and I came over as soon as I could. I knew they'd arrived early today. Ashley texted. Maybe they don't want anything to seem studied or rehearsed?"

Seth probably would have done both, writing a script for himself to practice in front of the mirror or over the phone with Mom and Lauren. He still hadn't shared the details with them. Their conversations stuck to updates about his nephews, a safer topic than his passion project. Lauren had never taken his search for Soupy seriously. He knew Lauren thought he'd invented everything and worried she would sway Mom to her side. And as the time passed without a sighting or solid evidence, he started to think she might be right. He had a chance to set the record straight, starting with his family.

He nodded.

"Okay." Elise blew out a sigh. "Pete will be conducting interviews and doing all the voice-over narration. From what I gather, they will film for the next six weeks. If they don't get results from the scientific work, they'll send someone here each month to conduct more research. But they'll be working on a script and how to structure the narrative of the story after they have all the footage."

Seth nodded. It was strange to think about someone filming him for a month and a half and then reshaping his past into a piece of entertainment.

"Pete is on his way over to conduct the first interview with you. This is the first of many. He has a list of questions, and I've reviewed it and agreed. It'll be like you're having a conversation with a friend. I promise."

"I trust you," Seth said. And he did. Slowly, he dropped his shoulders, and the tight coil in his gut loosened. Elise would look out for him, and he was grateful she'd agreed to manage him.

"Good," she smiled. "Because they are here." She pointed out the door.

Pete stood outside with a crew of four, waving.

Elise crossed to the door and held it open. "Please come in. Welcome."

Seth was rooted to his spot as a woman holding a boom mic, a man holding lights, a woman with a camera, and a man with a tackle box and two folding director's chairs entered and got to work inspecting the space.

"Seth! Great to see you," Pete said, his voice booming as he entered.

He looked perfect, flawless, in a pressed shirt with the most tailored puffy vest Seth had ever seen. As Pete neared, Seth saw he wore makeup.

Seth shook the outstretched hand. He'd probably be made up, too. He stared down at his typical flannel shirt and jeans. Would Seth have to wear this outfit during every interview for continuity? He could have picked something better, but they insisted on wanting him to be natural. Should he change? "Hello again."

"Sorry to burst in on you without too much notice. We," Pete pointed to Elise and then himself, "wanted to keep things casual today."

Elise smiled and nodded.

Seth relaxed. She'd make the right call on his behalf. Maybe this was better. With warning, he'd be nervous, and now he'd be himself.

"We're going to set up an area for the interview here." Pete pointed to the corner dedicated to Soupy, with merchandise neatly displayed. "If you don't mind, locking the door and lowering the shades?"

Seth nodded, not trusting his voice. He crossed to the front door, pulling the key from his pocket and lowering the blinds.

Elise joined him. "Just breathe," she murmured. "I'll be here the whole time. If you want to stop, just say so."

"Thanks," he said, again grateful for the warmth of her friendship and the strength he felt in having her with him.

"Seth? Can you come here really quick? We want to fix the lighting and get a little powder on you. Just enough so you won't shine on camera," Pete called.

Seth made his way to the corner and sat in the chair as directed. The makeup artist swabbed and swiped at his face. His nose itched, but he didn't dare touch it, content with wiggling the sneeze away.

"Alright," Pete said, clapping and rubbing his palms together. He sat in the chair across from Seth. "We're going to get started. We only have one camera today, so we're going to focus the spotlight on you for the entire interview. After we're done, we'll reposition the camera behind you to film me asking the same questions. You won't have to repeat yourself. Okay?"

Seth had no experience with any sort of filming and trusted their expertise. He flashed a thumbs-up.

"I'm going to jump right in without an introduction. It might seem a little jarring and out of order to skip small talk. But don't worry, we'll do a bunch of other interviews later to fill in the blanks. Editing will stitch everything together in the correct order. Ready?"

"Yes," he replied, his voice clear and steady.

"How can you think the creature in the lake is a mosasaurus?"

Seth gaped. He should have expected the question, but without preamble, it was jarring. "Why not?"

"Well, because there would be absolute carnage for starters. The lake would be red with blood, don't you think? A mosasaurus is a carnivore. Wouldn't body parts wash ashore? Skeletons might breakdown and turn the beach from a rocky shore to sand."

Yikes. Seth didn't like the grim image. "So are plesiosaurs," he countered. "It is almost accepted as fact that Nessie is a plesiosaur, and they are carnivorous. We have no reports of Nessie eating people.. Same with Soupy."

"Okay, point number two is that the species is extinct. How can you believe an animal that died off millions of years ago is still alive here?"

"The coelacanth found off Africa was supposed to be dead, too." Seth relaxed. He was well versed in defending Soupy to outsiders. While the questions were no-nonsense and direct, they sent Seth back to his comfort zone. "It's called the Lazarus effect. Plenty of species have been discovered that should be dead. And many more continue to be discovered. When you consider how much we don't know about the marine world, having a species survive in the wild is highly plausible. Avoiding detection is part of the magic of the creature."

"Is your research about magic or science?"

Seth arched a brow. "Why can't it be both? What's wrong with believing in the impossible?" He leaned forward. "Don't we all want a little magic?"

"You make a very compelling argument. But I have to ask, you have devoted your life to this search. You have quite the following worldwide and the support of your local community. How many times have you seen it?"

Seth held up three fingers. "Three encounters. Once, I saw its face. Twice, I've glimpsed its flippers."

"Take us back to the beginning."

"The first time I spotted it was while ice fishing with my dad," Seth said, stifling a shiver.

The chilly memory of that day lingered in his bones. He remembered the scent of woodsmoke curling in the dry air, the numbing cold that started at the soles of his feet and worked its way up his legs with hours on the frozen lake, and the cracking of the ice breaking through the long stretches of silence. "Under the ice," Seth began, "I spotted its eye and the corner of its massive jaw. The experience has stayed with me forever. I was too terrified to scream or react. I was powerless to move like I'd fallen through the hole into the lake."

"Brr," Pete gave an exaggerated shudder.

The over-the-top response didn't fit with Seth's story. A red light caught in his line of vision. He glanced at it, directly into the camera, and stiffened. He'd forgotten the interview was being filmed.

"But you continued to search?" Pete asked.

Seth nodded and focused on the other man, forcing his shoulders down. If Seth acted like they were having a normal conversation, he could speak without his vision blurring and his stomach churning.

"If you were scared, why continue to seek out the source of your nightmares?" Pete prodded.

"I never said nightmares. I've never had trouble sleeping. I wasn't just scared. The encounter was awe-inspiring, too. I had to know what I'd seen. I started spending all my free time at the library, reading every book I could find. Loon Lake Library has an extensive collection of books and articles about the fish and wildlife in the area. I came away disenchanted after every trip. Until a second-grade social studies unit on the dinosaurs. Then I spotted it. My creature. A mosasaurus."

"Why have remains never washed ashore? If, somehow, the creature does exist and has managed to avoid extinction, it would have to be living in some sort of pod or family structure, enough to reproduce. All living things die. Shouldn't we find a carcass? Bones?"

"The area is vast. Lake Superior is more of an ocean than a lake. The crew of the Edmund Fitzgerald was never found, and we knew where to look."

"CUT," Pete said. "Great stuff. Really, really good."

Seth glanced at Elise. She lifted her chin in the upward tilt of approval. His confidence grew. He could do this. He would make Dad proud.

* * *

Despite what the Lewises might believe, the Inn at Loon Lake was not the center of everyone's universe. Located on the lakeshore opposite the businesses, the inn was far enough away to make it avoidable for most citizens. The boardwalk was truly the heartbeat of the community. For today's meeting, however, the inn proved to be the centralized point between the sawmill, the tour company, and the inn.

Elise parked her car in the lot and crossed to the main entrance of the Victorian resort, pushing through the revolving front door and nodding her head to the staff she recognized as she made her way up the stairs to the top of the building.

Seth had done well. Extraordinarily well. Maybe the Soupy show wouldn't distract and cause chaos in the town. Maybe it would enhance tourism.

She needed to give him more credit. He was so easygoing and affable that she worried about the moments he could seem silly. When Pete started the interview, he had launched into combative questions. He hadn't allowed much time for Seth to pause and consider his answers. Not that Seth was particularly known for doing so, but still, he hardly had time to finish an answer before another verbal attack was fired.

Before the makeup, Seth had looked almost green. But he had recovered. Perhaps not having time to think was the key. He'd been totally natural and charming in his very specific way. The same way he'd convinced a whole town to encourage him despite the obvious doubts.

At the top of the stairs, Elise strode to the door at the end of the hall. She put her hands on either side of her waist and dragged in a deep breath. She never felt out of shape until she had to have a meeting at the inn. Once her breathing had returned to normal, she knocked on the door and waited, straining for a sound inside.

Waiting, pausing, considering. How would she have responded to the rapid-fire interview assault? Would she be put to the test? On camera? She shuddered.

The door opened.

Ashley appeared on the other side. "Good morning, Elise. Come on in, please. We're all here and ready for you."

Elise offered a tight smile and nodded. Growing up, Elise and Ashley had often been forced together because of their age and pushed apart because of their personality differences. Ashley thrived in chaos, but Elise needed order. Over the past year, they'd narrowed the distance between them, but still, a hesitation and awkwardness lingered in their newly forming friendship.

Elise entered the room and scanned the space.

A large partner's desk sat against one wall. Along both the front of the building and the back, two rows of windows let in streams of golden sunlight. It was like living in a magical tree-house. On a small area rug, two leather club chairs and a coffee table created a comfortable area to sit and chat. But today, folding chairs had been set up around the partner's desk to create a conference room atmosphere.

She nodded at Grant, Molly, Christopher, and Mr. Willie, the inn's groundskeeper. She was glad the groundskeeper had made it a priority to attend. She respected how busy his day-to-day schedule of physical labor kept him.

"Thank you all for taking the time to meet me. And thank you for accommodating the crew in the coach house," Elise said. "Really, it was very good of you."

Ashley waved off the gratitude. "Of course. It made sense."

"We are quite comfortable up here in the studio for the time being," Christopher said.

The studio was an apartment attached to the private offices at the top of the inn. "It's cozy," he added.

Ashley blushed. "We're always glad to help out a friend," she added.

"I'm sorry I'm late. I wasn't planning on listening to the entire interview," Elise said.

"How did it go?" Molly asked.

"Well. I think," Elise replied. "Who knows what the final product will be after they get all their footage and edit the whole investigation into some sort of story. But Seth did a great job."

"Of course he did," Grant said. "He's very comfortable in any circumstance."

"Interviews on camera can be tough, and this wasn't necessarily as relaxed as the morning shows that he did," Elise said. "Which brings us to our meeting. Thank you all for agreeing to let the TV crew set up equipment on your properties. You have the three best vantage points of the lake. The cameras will be left in position and will record nonstop for the next six weeks at minimum. Perhaps longer."

"I'll be curious what they pick up," Molly said.

Mr. Willie frowned. "Can we not get advance notice to

make ourselves available? Do they really need to record twenty-four seven?"

Elise considered the groundskeeper. He was not the most welcoming of men and was somewhat known for his gruff demeanor. But he shifted on his chair. "I'm sure the cameras on the inn's lighthouse will mostly catch birds flying over the lake. Not many are brave enough to swim in the chilly water. Nothing to be worried about."

"Takes away our privacy," Mr. Willie said.

"Don't worry, Mr. Willie," Ashley added. "They won't catch whatever deep, dark secret you must be hiding. I'm guessing it's water aerobics? I, for one, would love to catch a glimpse of that." She winked.

Mr. Willie growled and folded his arms over his chest.

"The TV crew is also interested in conducting on-camera interviews with each of you," Elise said.

"Us? Really?" Ashley asked. "What could we offer? Soupy is Seth's thing."

Elise shrugged. "If I get a heads-up on questions, I'll let you know. I'll be at every interview." She'd promised Seth she'd keep an eye on the project, and she meant it. While she didn't suspect anyone would purposely derail the investigation, she couldn't ever be sure of other people's motives.

She had learned long ago that governing other people was an impossibility. She couldn't get anyone to follow her rules. But she could mitigate the impact. And that was exactly what she'd do.

"I doubt I'd have anything much to say," Molly added. "I only just moved here."

"But we did have that boating accident last summer when we got stranded on the lake in the spot Seth calls the Timber Triangle. I'm sure you'll be asked to talk about your experiences," Grant said.

"Exactly," Elise agreed. "No one is going to try to get any of you to corroborate Soupy. How could you?"

The others all laughed.

Except for Mr. Willie, who wrinkled his brow further. "If that's all, I need to get to my rounds."

"Yes, of course. The cameras will be set up later today. If you have any issues, please call. And thank you all for supporting Seth in this," Elise said.

"I speak for everyone," Christopher said. "We'd do anything for Seth."

Elise smiled. She hoped it wouldn't come to that. With Soupy and with Seth, she stumbled into the unknown. "The fun run will be filmed. No one will be mic'd, but they have asked for waivers from all participants."

"Would you like us to handle that?" Ashley asked. "We can set up a table in the lobby for guests who are running, to facilitate checking in ahead of time."

Elise had wanted to avoid asking for more assistance. But she couldn't argue with the idea. The more runners pre-checked, the less hassle on race day. Not that she had many runners to worry about. She hadn't asked for help with the event, preferring to handle everything herself. For her trouble, she had fewer than fifty registrations.

Elise nodded. "Thank you. I'll have a booth at the event for the others to grab their race packets. If you could sign people in before the event, you'll make the morning a whole lot easier."

"Our pleasure," Christopher said. "Maybe we'll sell a few more spots once word gets out about the filming."

Elise hoped so. To hit her target, she needed at least one hundred and twenty-five runners. With only a few days to go, the feat seemed impossible.

Seth hadn't been deterred by her low numbers. He'd printed two hundred stickers. He'd refused payment, too.

She'd forced him to sell her the stickers at cost to avoid the appearance of impropriety. She was touched by the gesture.

"I'll be happy to help on race day so you can worry about....everything else," Molly said.

"Me too," Grant chimed in. "I'm not a runner. You should enjoy your event as much as you're able."

Elise's cheeks burned. "I appreciate all of you. I'll stop by later today with waivers and race packets. We have four days until the race. It'll be an all hands on deck situation."

"Those are terms I definitely understand." Grant chuckled. "We've got your back."

"Thank you." Her gratitude was genuine and her delivery a little breathless. Tears stung her eyes. Once again, she found herself relying on others as things slipped through her grasp. She wasn't fully in control. But she could trust these people, a tiny bit, with these easy tasks. She had no choice.

Chapter Six

Four days later, Seth crossed one arm in front of his chest and reached for his shoulder blade with his opposite hand. And then he repeated the process on the other side. He hadn't voluntarily exercised or stretched since high school. Gym class wasn't a choice.

He dropped his arms to his sides and rolled his neck, scanning the crowd. It was sizeable. Men, women, and children dressed in athletic gear filled the grass around him. Flashes of bright lime green from Soupy Fun Run sweatbands on every wrist added to the anticipation of the event.

Traditionally, the race started at the Hale family plot, on the hill overlooking the lake halfway between the museum and the inn. The race paused at Scoops, There It Is, where the entrants downed milkshakes before running back up the deceptively steep hill. Whoever made it to the top without getting sick was declared the winner.

To accommodate a crowd, modifications had been made. Specifically, Mr. Willie refused to spend all day hosing off the path. A tent had been set up at the end of the race to serve dishes of Zach's small-batch ice creams to all finishers.

Another tent at the start was ready for racers who still needed to pick up their numbers, stickers, and sign the waivers.

The TV crew was positioned throughout the course to film the event. Pete promised he'd focus his cameras on the locals who would be participating in the interviews. Molly, Grant, Ashley, Zach, Lonnie, Elise, and Seth.

Mr. Willie had almost disappeared into thin air. He did that a lot. He sort of popped up where and when he was needed. Seth had long admired the skill of appearing as if summoned by thought and vanishing before being asked to leave. Seth would have to ask Mr. Willie his secrets.

The cell phone vibrated in the band on Seth's bicep. He'd lost his wireless headphones on the drive over but decided to keep the phone in place in case he was needed. He slipped the phone out of the holster and accepted the call.

"Seth?" Mom asked the moment the line connected.

"Hi, Mom."

"I got him, Lauren," Mom called, her voice muffled.

Oh no. He glanced around, eager for a valid excuse to hang up and avoid one of their tag-team calls.

"Seth? What is this news about a movie crew following you around?" His younger sister demanded. She'd been bossy and competitive since birth. Involved in every sport, she'd often been on the go with Mom as her chauffeur.

If Seth was being honest, he'd been glad for a bit of freedom from either's watchful eye. But the trade-off was the combined force of their scrutiny on phone calls and visits.

"Oh, yeah. Sorry," Seth said. "I forgot."

"Honey, how do you forget something big like a film you're starring in?" Mom asked.

Her tone was concerned, juxtaposing with Lauren's judgment.

"It's not a big budget blockbuster for theaters next summer," he said, his cheeks burning. Was anyone nearby eavesdropping? He didn't want to downplay the significance of the project nor did he want to overinflate his role. "A very nice TV production company approached me about filming."

"And you didn't tell us? Did you get hit on the head?" Mom asked.

"I'm fine, Mom. Promise. I guess I forgot because everything happened so quickly, and I'm still pinching myself." He sighed. "I didn't tell you because I wasn't sure it was real. Since filming started, everything has been nonstop and busy. I haven't had too much free time to think. When I'm home, I'm exhausted."

"And you're not making calls," Lauren said, her voice dripping with sarcasm. "We get it. You don't want to add us to the cast list. We're not part of it."

"Hush," Mom said. "The search was never our thing. Always Dad and Seth's. I'm guessing this is about Soupy?"

"Thanks, Mom. Yes, it is. And I am sorry I didn't tell you. Just an oversight. Nothing malicious. The production company is taking a very thorough approach to searching the lake. I'm sure they'll find him."

"You have nothing to prove to anyone," Lauren said in her no-nonsense tone. She always hovered between being critical and caring. "You matter. You're a big part of the community, and you don't have to do something huge to be remembered. Everyone who gets to have you in their life is lucky."

"That's not what I'm doing," he replied by rote. A lump of emotion caught in his throat. If he was only seeking success for himself, he'd listen to his sister. But what he searched for went beyond him. He wanted to memorialize his dad. Brian Boyd deserved to be remembered alongside the other great figures in Loon Lake's history. Seth would make sure Dad was.

"What happens next? After you get your answers, you'll stop?" Lauren asked. "You'll focus on the printshop?"

He had no reply. He'd never thought about what came

after finding Soupy. With his focus dedicated to one purpose and his life fully in the before, he'd never stopped to consider the after.

"Dad would be so proud," Mom said with a sniff. "We're proud, too. And no, Lauren. He'll continue educating and advocating for the lake and all its inhabitants. Dad always believed the search would lead to big things for you."

"Thanks, Mom." He smiled and glanced up the hill.

Elise met his gaze and waved.

As always, she was a sight for his sore eyes. With her smoothed bun and fitted workout clothes, she was always impeccable. Her perfection was a constant. She anchored him more than she could know.

"At least tell me Elise is involved," Lauren said.

Seth's skin burned. "Yes. She is."

"Oh, that is good," Mom replied. "She's so sensible. I'm glad she's helping."

"I need to get going," Seth said.

"But you'll stay in touch?" Mom asked.

"I will do my best. Love you both," he said.

"Love you," Mom and Lauren said in unison, their voices almost perfect copies of one another.

He ended the call and slipped the phone back into his armband. He crossed the distance to Elise. "Hey," he called as he neared. "I was finishing a call with Mom. How's it all going over here? You've managed to attract quite a crowd."

"I left the inn in charge of the last-minute registrations and organization," Elise said, twisting her head from one side to the other.

In casual exercise gear, meant for sweating and not her typical look, she shouldn't be the most beautiful woman in the vicinity. Somehow, she always was. He admired how she was never thrown for a loop or that she never questioned whether or not she belonged.

"I'm very impressed. I had no idea Ashley could deliver on her promise for more people."

"Never bet against her," Seth said with a smile. "I'm glad I made two hundred stickers. I've handed them all out. I did spend quite a bit of time talking Zach off a ledge about how he'd get enough ice cream to serve everybody."

Elise rolled her eyes. "I don't have much sympathy for him. Did you know he tried to upsell the cost? He wanted to make a profit."

"Don't you remember when he auctioned himself off as a prom date in high school? He thought he'd make a lot of money. Fast. And get a girlfriend. His foolproof plan."

Elise laughed, throwing back her head for a spontaneous second. "I forgot about that." She placed her hands on either side of her waist.

Seth felt tingly and warm, like he wanted to bask in her glow. All day. Every day. He didn't want the moment to end. "He ended up alone and still broke."

"Well, no worries there." She sobered up, straightening and schooling her features into their usual calm expression.

Usually, he'd berate himself for killing the moment by pushing for more. But this time, he saw the hint of a smile in her eyes.

"I've hit our fundraising target with the sign-up fees for the fun run," she said. "The parade won't have any donations tied to it. I won't make another financial appeal for the foundation until year-end. I need to deliver quality experiences so everyone has fond memories and wants to support more opportunities."

"You will. Starting today," Seth said. "Are you ready to run?"

She shrugged. "I'm not much of a runner. I'm sure this first half will be fine, but I'm already anticipating I'll be walking up the hill."

"You're not trying to earn a medal?"

She shook her head.

"Really? I remember you being pretty good at sports in school," he said, as evenly as he could. He was shocked. Why else did Elise pursue such painstaking perfection if not to win?

"I don't need accolades for physical accomplishments."

He did. Not necessarily for running a race, but to prove he was capable. He'd take any award he could. Best printer in the North Woods. Most original graphic designer in the state. Even the temporary flag of bestseller on his ebooks at the online retailer stores had been a very welcome validation.

A bright light caught in his gaze, and he turned. He spotted the TV crew angling a light and the camera in his direction. But no boom mic, thankfully.

"Oh, right," Elise said, stiffening. "I almost forgot about filming."

"At least we aren't mic'd today," Seth said. "I don't think anyone wants to hear heavy breathing as we huff and puff our way through the course."

She grinned. "That's a good point. You were great on camera. I'm nervous about my turn in the hot seat. Do you have any tips?"

"Once I focused on Pete and had a normal conversation with him, it was easy. That's the key. Act normal. Ignore the equipment. The camera isn't there."

She nodded. "You are a natural on screen. You did great on all of those morning shows, too." She extended her arms to either side. "This crowd is due to you. You've brought a lot of attention to Loon Lake."

He studied the crowd once again, seeing it for the first time. He had done this, boosted tourism by sharing his story. Maybe that was enough. Maybe if all the cameras and investigative research was completed and they found out Soupy was an overgrown eel or something else, Seth would still have value. He was worth more than his monster.

"On your marks," Ashley said over a loudspeaker. "Get set..."

"Will you stick with me?" he asked Elise.

"Always."

"GO!"

* * *

Barreling down the grassy hill on a bright and sunny day, Elise felt like she was flying. And she laughed. She hadn't felt so exuberant and free since childhood. Back then, she used to love to race down the hills, running in the spring with kites flying behind her, sledding in the winter and turning at the last second to land in a snowbank and not the lake, roller-skating in the summer to cool off with a self-made breeze, and—her favorite—using the speed from running downhill to launch herself into a pile of leaves in the autumn. She hadn't done any of those things in years. She hadn't spared a thought or realized what she was missing. She hadn't lied to Seth. She wasn't a runner.

But maybe she could seek out more fun.

He ran next to her and, every so often, turned and smiled.

Her stomach knotted up every time. He was so kind and so engaging. It was a dangerous combination. He'd be easy to love. She couldn't let herself fall for him.

*Or what? What's the worst that'll happen? You'll have real, lasting love with the best person you've ever known?*

She swallowed a groan as her inner monologue taunted her.

"Are you okay? Do you want to slow down?" Seth asked between shallow breaths.

"I'm fine. Let's keep going," she said. If she focused on her pace and her steps, she remained in the present and not lost in her reveries.

The Soupy Fun Run had been meticulously organized. Elise was both surprised and nonplused. With the proper motivation, Ashley could achieve anything. She was clever, creative, capable, and charming. The trouble was getting her to focus and finish. Elise was pleased with the result, and that she hadn't needed to micromanage the situation at all.

Maybe she didn't need to be the boss at all times. Maybe she could count on others to do their share. Then she could do something like fall in love for real.

She gulped. What would it be like if she was vulnerable with another person? What if she told Seth what she felt for him and how her feelings had deepened over the years? Since high school, she'd sort of liked him from afar. Their graduating class of seventy-five meant they'd been together for so much of their educational years that they all shared a connection, whether they liked it or not.

She'd never been flashy or popular. She always liked to observe and study, taking mental notes to analyze later and never speaking without a lot of thought. But Seth had always been free with his words. While others speaking without thinking often led to hurt feelings, he had never addressed another person with anything less than joy and openness.

To others, he might seem innocent or naive. She only saw a man with a pure soul and encouraging smile. While she was prickly and cold, he was soft and warm. Did opposites really attract? Would it make sense to the community at large?

*Why should I care?*

Running down the grassy hill in a crowd, Elise synced her pace with Seth, and the hairs on her left arm, the side closest to him, stood perfectly on end. His nearness was a delicious torture. She forgot why she cared what others would think of their pairing.

The town had seen and withstood worse than the pairing of a grumpy gal and Loon Lake's sunshine son. Last year, after Xavier Hale's sudden death of natural causes, his daughter had nearly been killed in a very unnatural way after abduction by a father and son now serving life sentences in jail. When she—and everyone else—thought the drama had quieted down, a pyromaniac lawyer who had been in league with the nefarious family duo of the earlier incident tried to steal and murder for his own success.

In light of those scandals, and the normal tidbits of gossip shared in a tight-knit town, would her pursuit of Seth really even draw any attention?

"I bet you do win a medal," he said, leaning close.

His breath on her cheek was a warm invitation. She licked her suddenly dry lips. Should she accept?

"I think we lost our camera crew," he said.

"Did we?" She frowned and stiffened. She'd forgotten about the extra sets of eyes trained on them. He'd told her to relax and be natural. That was easy for him because everything was easy for him. Seth moved through life like a jellyfish. He seemed to float on the current, yet he reached a destination of his own choosing every time.

Could she emulate him?

"Okay, last few yards and then we turn, are you ready?" he asked.

"No," she answered truthfully. "But I'll walk uphill for ice cream any day."

He grinned. "Same."

And in truth, maybe that was part of his secret to enjoying the most of life. Simple pleasures were the most fundamental. All she had to do was trust others. She wasn't sure that was entirely possible. But she wanted to try.

At the top of the hill, a hundred yards away, Molly and Grant paced under the canopy for day-of registrations.

A dull ache settled low in Elise's gut. She knew the sensation. It meant *what now* and often accompanied her after she delegated a task.

"Looks like I won't be running or walking the rest of the race today." She hated cutting time with her friend short. Instinct, however, propelled her to march straight to the problem. "If you'll excuse me?" she whispered to Seth and turned toward the booth.

But Seth wasn't discouraged. After a few steps, he caught up with her.

She felt his gaze on her back and was more glad for the company than she would admit, but she didn't acknowledge him as she purposefully strode to the table. "What's wrong?" she asked the anxious pair, keeping her voice hushed.

Molly's face was red and puffy.

Grant shook his head. "The waivers. We had them with us. And then suddenly. Poof." He snapped his fingers.

"Ooohhhhkkkkaayy..." Elise stalled as she darted her gaze here, there, and everywhere. Papers didn't vanish. Why? Who would want them besides the production company? The wind might have blown the table clear. Or a helpful bystander might have cleaned up and tossed them in the trash.

But she didn't see any sheets on the grass. Nor did she spot a trash can anywhere close. The garbage had been moved to encircle Zach's ice cream stand and prevent littering. The disappearance was probably more likely a misunderstanding than a mystery. "You had the waivers from this morning. Not all of them. So I—"

"We had them all," Molly blurted. She pressed her hands to her red cheeks. "Elise, I'm so sorry. Ashley dropped off the banker's box full of waivers she'd collected at the inn. We had everyone cleared to appear on camera, even spectators. We thought we'd save you the trouble of going to the inn by having all the forms together in one place."

"Oh." The single-word response was half verbal, half breath. Elise had no desire to hurt anyone's feelings. Molly had been caring enough to volunteer so Elise could enjoy the event.

In the end, the worst-case scenario, something so outlandish Elise wouldn't have even imagined it, played out. The box went missing.

Elise didn't blame Molly or Grant. She held herself accountable. Elise always paid attention to details. She didn't expect others to understand how important every task was. Now she was proven correct again. It was easier to sacrifice her time and energy than to delegate to the unprepared. "I'm sure someone grabbed the box by mistake. There is no other reasonable explanation. We just need to find it."

Grant snapped again. "Yes, Mr. Willie stopped by a little while ago. I went to the bathroom, and Molly got ice cream. Mr. Willie might have grabbed it by accident, trying to start the tear down so the inn's grounds can get back to normal. I'll find him." Grant ran off toward the ice cream tent.

"I'll go with him and check the other tent. I'm so sorry. I can't believe this happened," Molly said, her voice cracking.

Elise shook her head and held up a hand. "No apologies necessary. Accidents happen." *Not to me, usually, but to others.*

With a nod, Molly ran after Grant.

Seth leaned close. "You're very calm. What's the damage if the waivers are gone?"

Elise sighed and faced him, taking a half step back. He was very close, confidently taking up her personal space. And she didn't mind. He was a solid wall of muscle she could lean on. That was tempting. But she couldn't give in when she potentially ruined his big moment.

She scanned their surroundings, making sure no one lurked nearby.

The crowd gathered around the ice cream tent. A few stragglers crossed the finish line. But they were, for all intents and purposes, alone. *In plain sight,* she reminded herself.

"We promised the production crew we'd have this event all sorted so it could be filmed. I don't know how much they would have used even with the proper permissions in place. Blurring nearly every face in a crowd seems like a tedious task. But it does feel like we broke a promise to them. That's not a good start to our partnership," she said.

Seth looked solemn and serious.

Elise hated to worry him. She didn't want to voice her fears and make them his. Without the footage of the community, she worried the film would be too hyper-focused on Seth. Would his character be twisted into something silly? Comedic? He had the town's loyalty. That had to translate on film. He needed the community to show up and do their part on camera.

"The worst that can happen," Seth began, "is they blur the faces in the crowd and focus on us. Not so bad."

*Isn't it?* The project was Seth's, not hers. Her part created a snafu. She didn't want her participation to ruin anything.

"Found them," Molly shouted from a few yards away.

Elise stared past Seth at Molly, pointing at Mr. Willie.

The groundskeeper carried the banker's box, scowling all the way.

"Crisis averted," Elise said, feigning enthusiasm. "Thanks for keep a good perspective on everything."

Seth looked like he wanted to say something.

Was he about to comment on her use of the word crisis? Her panic at being zoomed in on by the cameras? Her life becoming a storyline? Luckily, she didn't need to explain herself. Because she didn't have answers.

*Chapter Seven*

Seth strode into the inn's lobby the next day with a stack of brochures to restock the rack near the front desk. Without a true visitor center, the inn became the go-to destination for tourists seeking information about local attractions. The tour boats and local businesses all had fliers in the magazine rack. Until this summer, however, Seth had no personal stake in the placement. He produced brochures, fliers, and postcard pamphlets for everyone but had nothing to advertise himself. Once his memoir took off, he'd decided to approach the inn about displaying information about Soupy and how to report sightings. Christopher and Ashley encouraged the idea.

Seth had to make weekly trips to restock. Not that he minded. He was always glad for a chance to catch up with the Lewises. And today, with a little bit of a heavy heart, he was hoping for a run-in with one Lewis in particular.

He finished inserting the pamphlets and straightened the other marketing materials, making a note to let the boardwalk businesses know that their coupons were running low and nearing expiration.

"Oh, Seth," Ashley said as she descended the stairs. "Hi. Nice to see you."

He slowly rose, grateful for his timing. "Hi, Ashley. How are you?"

"Busy." She chuckled. "As always. But today I'm really in a rush. I'm being interviewed by your TV crew, and I have to get ready."

"Oh." He frowned. So much for thinking he was in the right place at the right time. He gripped the box tight. "Sure. Thank you for participating."

"It's my pleasure." She flashed her trademark grin before her gaze narrowed, focusing on his face. "What's wrong?"

"I was hoping to have a word with you, but it's not a good time. Never mind." He turned.

She stopped him with a hand on his shoulder. "Of course we can chat. I'll always make time for you," she said. "Would you like to join me for breakfast?"

"Now?" He hated to barge in and shakeup her whole day.

"No time like the present. I really should eat a proper meal today, or I'll be sort of jittery and jumpy on camera from surviving off coffee."

His stomach growled.

She grinned and reached for his empty box. "Great. Kim? Can you recycle this for me, please?" she asked one of the workers behind the desk. "Thank you." She handed over the box and tipped her head to the restaurant across the lobby.

He remained in awe of the confidence with which she moved through the world. She never questioned whether or not she belonged. Why would she? Here, at the inn, she owned the place.

The maître d led the pair to a table in the corner near the window, pulling out a chair for the boss.

Seth settled himself and accepted a menu with a nod. Elise's air of self-assurance was even more impressive to him because she wasn't a legacy. She couldn't fall back on her family name like Ashley. Elise had to be enough on her own. And she was so much more than a steward of something great, passing it from one generation to the next. She charted her own destiny.

A server filled Ashley's coffee cup and brought a glass of cola for Seth.

He widened his eyes and met Ashley's gaze.

"We like to take care of our regulars here," she said again with that poise of being in charge, "french toast?"

He licked his lips.

"Two orders and a side of home fries," she told the server. "Thank you."

The server nodded, grabbed the menus, and walked away.

"I'm glad to have an excuse to sit down and eat real food," she said. "You can't imagine how many days I run around and survive off granola bars when we have a world-class restaurant under our roof. It's such a shame."

"Thank you for bringing me. I haven't eaten here in probably a year."

"Really? You are always welcome to be my guest," she said. "Thanks for letting us expand into the Soupy fun run. The guests really enjoyed it."

"I'm glad. I was hoping with so many eyes, we'd get a sighting of Soupy, but I suppose the weather conditions were too sunny for him."

"Or her," she said.

He sipped his drink, enjoying the pop and fizz of bubbles on his tongue.

"What's up? I can tell something is bugging you."

"You can?"

"Sure. I've never known you to be so serious and quiet."

"I have questions for you, but I don't know how to ask them without offending you."

"Oh," she sipped her coffee and set the cup on its saucer. "Well, I suppose tone determines interpretation and intent. But you always look for the best in others. I don't think you'll be accusing me of anything, so go ahead and ask."

He dragged in a shaky breath and set his drink on the white-linen covered table, interlacing his icy fingers. "I'm worried about the whole TV thing."

"You are? I thought you wanted it. Elise said you were great on camera."

"She did?"

Ashley nodded. "Elise is hardly one for exaggeration."

That was very true. She only said what she absolutely meant. Or she didn't open her mouth.

"How does this offend me?" Ashley asked.

"My concern is that they won't find anything out there. And I wanted to know how you did it."

"Did what?" She propped her chin with her hand, resting both elbows on the table.

"Keep going with your ghost when no one believed you. Why didn't you just give up?"

"Ah." She folded her arms over her chest. "Okay, I understand, and no, I'm not offended." She sipped her coffee again. "When I first came back, I slipped into the lighthouse and pretended to be a ghost. Christopher saw through it immediately. But I had several firsthand encounters with a spirit out there." She pressed a hand to her heart. "I know it in here that there is a ghost, a lost soul, a spirit, whatever you want to call a benevolent haunt. I don't need anyone else to believe me because I know it's true."

The server approached with their orders and set the food in front of them. The rich smells of buttery, cinnamon, sugary goodness wafted up, encircling their table with heavenly scents.

"Thank you," she said to the server and sliced off a piece of her toast.

Seth nodded at the server as he walked away and considered Ashley's words. She wasn't the type of person to need outside validation. How did he emulate her? As far as he could tell, he was trapped in a loop. To not care about others' opinions, he had to establish himself with something big. Like finding Soupy.

"Are you alright? Is the order okay?" She asked, her words muffled from behind a napkin.

"I'm great." He sliced off a corner, dipped the toast in the warm syrup, and ate, savoring the bite. "This is delicious."

"Thank you. We have a wonderful kitchen staff." She set her fork to the side and interlaced her hands on the table. "Don't get discouraged, and don't give up. We all support you no matter what. Soupy has already given so much to this town."

"Thanks, that's kind of you to say."

She waved off the gratitude. "I'm confident the cameras will find something. Soupy the Mosasaurus can't stay hidden for long with such coordinated strategies. Cameras by land and by lake, the boat tours, and the experiments? We'll catch him, and you'll be huge news." Her eyes sparkled with excitement.

*And then what do I do? What happens next?*

Lauren's comment slammed into him like Zach's truck on an icy day. Suddenly, his sister's words weren't discouraging as much as illuminating. If he reached the end of the journey, he'd need a new path. And he wanted to keep Soupy safe. "I don't want any experiments conducted on him. He needs protection as an endangered species. I worry finding Soupy might mean pain."

"Yeah, you have a valid point," Ashley said. "Finding a living dinosaur is, forgive the cliché, uncharted waters. Who knows what might happen. Do you think anyone could capture the creature? She's gone undetected for so long. Her stealth skills established her survival."

"I don't know. With all the government resources behind the endeavor, anything is possible." He forked another bite of french toast and chewed. The sugary breakfast soured on his tongue.

She blew across her coffee and took a thoughtful sip.

Ashley's mind worked fast, developing wonderful ideas in a flash. She had the faraway look in her eyes again. She set the mug in the saucer. "Might I once again suggest the children's story angle? If you go the way of Puff the Magic Dragon, you'd endear the creature to a legion of young fans. Kids are a powerful force for change. They will help you be a voice for Soupy. And then you can also get to work lobbying politicians for safeguards."

She had an answer for everything. A year ago, when she had returned to town, she had tried to steer him onto a path of children's literature. But he'd been determined to write his memoir. Now, he understood the significance of what she was saying. She wanted to help him make an impact. Seth smiled. He wasn't sure why his sister's words had rankled him. He only needed to talk through his problems with a friend to find the solutions.

Of course, everything depended on Soupy the Mosasaurus. If he or she was anything less, everyone would be disappointed. Especially Dad's memory. Seth wouldn't let that happen.

* * *

Standing on the beach at the inn, Elise gazed across the water, inhaling the fresh scent of mineral-rich water and rocks. The perfume of Loon Lake was her own personal aromatherapy. She found calm and healing at the edge of the water.

Yesterday, after the run, she had changed and met with the crew to oversee the installation of cameras around town. The devices were small and unobtrusive. If she hadn't seen where they'd be installed, she wouldn't know anything was out of the ordinary.

Which was part of what Pete and Kate wanted. Elise had met up with the producer pair. They were pleased with the footage so far, liking Seth's screentime most of all. They were eager to tackle more interviews to put together a rough cut for the networks they were pitching the project to.

Elise didn't quite understand how any of it was meant to work. Until they completed their research, what could they sell? A show about the town? Loon Lake wasn't a particularly special or unique place. Didn't audiences prefer to watch shows about folks living large? The flashiest car in town was a three-year-old SUV. Even the local millionaire, Grant, who had sold his start-up to a major tech company, was a fairly unassuming person.

What—besides Soupy—could be of any interest to a network? Maybe she didn't want to know. She had gotten help with the fun run, and—after the snafu—that event had gone well. She'd enjoyed herself more than she had in a long time. She hadn't been working through a detailed timeline or never-ending checklist. She had shown up and participated.

She was hoping to do that again today.

"Hey, I heard you were down here," Ashley called as she crossed the lawn. "Before we get started with the TV crew, can I get you anything?"

"Me?" Elise poked herself in the chest with a pointer finger. "I'm not the one who will be on camera."

Ashley shrugged. "Hospitality is a way of life. Are you sure? An iced tea, perhaps?"

Elise shook her head. She'd already had too much caffeine for the day. The clock had struck two as she'd left the museum to drive over to the inn. Any tea would keep her up all night, and she needed every moment of rest she could get.

"Okay, then, if you change your mind, wave down one of the servers or beach attendants, and they can help you." Ashley rubbed her palms together. "I can't seem to warm up today."

Elise was surprised. With no clouds overhead and no breeze, the seventy-three degrees might as well have been ninety. It was one of the warmest days so far in a mild summer.

"Is there anything I need to know before the interview? Anything to go over?" Ashley asked, twisting a strand of her hair around a finger and nibbling her bottom lip.

Ashley was nervous? About talking? Elise could have been knocked over by a feather. Since when did Ashley not have a witty remark at the ready? Elise shook her head. "Nothing to review. Just relax and have a conversation with Pete. He's the host of the show and the interviewer."

Ashley nodded.

"Did I hear my name?" Pete called, cupping both hands around his mouth as he neared with the usual crew and Kate. He extended a hand to Ashley and then to Elise. "Great to meet you, Mrs. Hale-Lewis, and nice to see you again, Elise."

Was Elise imagining the tightness in his greeting? Probably. The waivers had been discovered before the production company was alerted to the disappearance. The morning had gone well. Any sudden change in his demeanor must be her projection.

"Please, call me Ashley. I'll feel like I'm a thousand years old if you're on a first-name basis with everyone else in town but calling me missus," Ashley said and chuckled.

"A pleasure, Ashley," Pete said.

Did his eyes twinkle? Elise expected the response from the introduction. Everyone loved Ashley.

"This is Kate, our producer," Pete continued. "She wanted to observe today's interview. If that's alright?"

Ashley shot Elise a questioning look.

Elise appreciated the deference. "Yes. Of course."

"Great. So, first we'd like to do our interview, and then we thought you could give us a tour of the property?" Pete asked.

"I can give you a tour of the lighthouse, definitely. But we'll need to coordinate a visit for the rest of the grounds with Mr. Willie. He's our groundskeeper and oversees the entire property. It's his domain, we all just live in it," Ashley said with a smile.

"We set up the chairs on the island to get this beautiful backdrop," Kate said. "Shall we go there now?"

Ashley nodded and led the way, falling into an easy chat with Pete. Like they were old friends.

Elise lurked near the back of the group, marveling at Ashley's ease. Like Seth, the woman never met a stranger and immediately clicked with every person she came across. What a gift.

"Surprised to see you here," Kate said, leaning towards Elise as they walked over the bridge.

*I could say the same.* Elise would err on the side of surprise and not indignation. "Oh?"

"I know you're managing Seth, but I didn't think you'd be present for every interview."

"Why?" Elise folded her arms over her chest and tilted her head to the side. "It was clearly stated in the contract that I be permitted at every on-camera interaction."

"Of course, I assumed that was a formality. You have other demands on your time. What about the parade? You must have a lot to do."

Elise gritted her teeth. The remark was too pointed to

ignore. "It won't be the rose parade." She forced a laugh. "We have plenty of trucks and flatbeds to do the day justice."

"If you're needed elsewhere..." Kate said.

*Not so fast.* Elise wouldn't be pushed out of her role, overseeing the interviews. "I promised Seth I'd keep an eye on things. And I'm curious."

"About?"

"What you'll ask. No one has ever claimed to see Soupy besides Seth." Elise shrugged. "I'm wondering how other people will be relevant to the discussion. I'd imagine the research will be the main driver of the project."

"We'll see," Kate said before moving ahead to stand next to the camera operator.

Elise fought a shudder. Was that supposed to be a threat? No, she couldn't read danger in every situation. She stopped at the side of the new lighthouse, letting the warmth of the sunbaked white painted bricks radiate into her skin.

"Three, two, one," the camera operator called.

"First off," Ashley said as the camera started rolling. "I've never seen Soupy. I'm not sure what I can tell you. I hate to be a disappointment."

"You could never be considered that," Pete said.

Ashley smiled.

The gregarious pair had an undeniable chemistry, not necessarily romantic but something worth watching. It was very different from Seth's earnest interview the other day.

"I like to be upfront with people," Ashley held her hands palms up.

"Much appreciated. You grew up here in Loon Lake."

"At this inn. It's been in my family since the town's founding. Over the years, we've expanded and renovated. Like many other citizens, I'm the latest generation continuing a legacy. We have deep roots here."

"And you've never seen anything on the water?" Pete

asked. "In your entire life, you've witnessed nothing amiss on the surface?"

Ashley shook her head. "I believe Seth. But no, I've never seen Soupy."

"That's not quite what I asked," Pete countered. "Have you ever encountered anything out of the ordinary? Loon Lake seems like a special, almost magical place."

"It's not Brigadoon," Ashley said with a laugh.

Pete chuckled. "No, but you know what I mean. The inn is a historic, grand building. This lighthouse seems new."

"It is new. A fire a year ago destroyed the original building. Of course, that lighthouse was never operational. It was built as a folly for tourists to enjoy in the twenties."

"A hundred years ago?"

"Yes. The building wasn't as well constructed as the inn and fell into disrepair within a few decades. Which was a shame. The fact it survived as long as it did was almost a miracle. I hate to lose any piece of our history. But the new lighthouse is sturdier and bigger, accommodating more visitors who want to climb to the top for an unparalleled view of the lake."

Pete nodded. "I imagine a lot of Soupy fanatics will make the climb. You mentioned a fire?"

"Well. A fire and an explosion, and then another fire."

"And that's not out of the ordinary?"

"Maybe the first fire." Ashley's little giggle was contagious. "If it happens twice, it starts an unfortunate pattern."

Elise studied the cheerful faces of the crew, reflecting back the enthusiasm of the interviewee. She could understand trying to make light of a painful situation to cope. But doing so on camera shocked Elise. A pit formed low in her stomach.

What was happening? How had Pete steered Ashley into this conversation? Should Elise intervene? But how and why? Nothing Ashley said was untrue, but it also didn't reflect the real gravity of the situation. And above all, this topic had nothing to do with Soupy. It was airing the town's dirty laundry for all to see.

Elise glanced at Kate. With her shoulders back and a broad grin on her face, she was clearly fine with the direction of the interview and seemed almost eager for it. *This is Seth's moment*. Elise willed Ashley to remember the reason for the documentary.

"I believe a ghost sparked the first fire," Ashley said, utterly sober, her face the very picture of sincerity. All mirth drained from her exuberant mannerisms. She held still and steady, making unflinching eye contact with Pete.

Kate's grin stretched further.

Elise had been feeling like she could take a step back and trust other people. Like she didn't need to always be the leader. Sure, the waivers had been a temporary setback. But their swift discovery reassured Elise that she could trust others.

But this interview? How had the team learned about Ashley's ghost? And the fire? Elise did her best to conceal last summer's drama. Pete steered the conversation with expert precision. Like he knew everything. Someone had talked. Who?

Elise was powerless to stop Ashley or rein her in. She'd have to do her best to mitigate the damage of this conversation. Ashley's supernatural talk created the sort of sideshow Elise did not want. Ashley had somehow jumped into Seth's project and stolen the spotlight. The worst part would be that Seth wouldn't mind, not if he thought he was helping a friend be heard, even at his own expense.

"Tell me more about the ghost," Pete said.

Elise gripped her elbows, tight, and held on. She'd deal with the fallout after she had all the facts. And—no doubt— she was in for a long wait as Ashley would make the most of a chance for her embellished story with a rapt audience.

*Chapter Eight*

Loon Lake wasn't known for its parades.

As Seth added the final flourish to his float, a splash of red paint to the jaws of the cardboard and paper-mache Soupy, he had to wonder why not. Making the float had been fun, even after all the late nights. He stretched his creative muscles in a different medium. With so much of his day spent designing on a computer or in a sketchbook, he had a lot of trial and error in bringing his vision to life in three dimensions. The mostly gray mosasaurus wasn't perfect. He'd developed a better technique for sculpting the cardboard with the wet strips of newspaper as he'd worked further down the body. If he had more time, he'd smooth the shape and refine it into a better representation. But he was pleased with his effort and couldn't wait to wave to the kids from alongside his creation as Zach pulled the Soupy float.

"Wow, this looks great," Zach called, crossing the strip mall parking lot. "You've done a lot without much notice. Kind of wild to throw a huge event and expect everyone to help out." He clapped a hand on Seth's shoulder.

Seth appreciated the praise but not the hint of criticism.

Elise had an idea, and he was glad to help her. That was more than friendship. That was community.

"Thanks for your help. I'm not sure I'd be good at steering with this behind me," Seth said.

Zach shrugged. "It's not a big deal. I've hauled bigger cargo. Besides, you've done a good job. If anything goes wrong, it won't be a reflection on you."

Seth frowned. Zach's comment was like a pre-apology. For what? *Can Zach see the future? Is he having déjà vu?* "Why would something go wrong?"

Zach held up his hands, palms facing out. "I'm just saying. Accidents happen."

*Not to Elise.* "Well..." Seth dragged the word. "I disagree. I am sort of responsible for how the parade goes. Elise invited me to be involved in her event for the sake of the cameras. We needed more to film. I can't let her down. If something goes wrong, she'll look bad, but I'd feel terrible."

"You won't. What a marvel of cardboard and ingenuity. Come on, let's get going before we're late."

Seth walked around the flatbed, double-checking that everything was well secured for the drive.

Zach attached the trailer to his truck and hopped in the driver's seat.

Satisfied with his handiwork, Seth climbed into the cab. "Are you okay? What happened with Mary? I never asked. I'm sorry."

"Nothing. Fine. It's fine." Zach kept his gaze on the road.

Mary must have told Zach they had no chance. Seth wouldn't try to comfort or commiserate until Zach opened up. But Seth felt bad. Mary was nice and down-to-earth. She brought out the same qualities in Zach.

With hazard lights flashing, Zach slowly rolled toward town. He checked his mirrors and waved at honking cars in a ceaseless loop.

Seth often thought Zach would be a good mayor. Like many things in Loon Lake, the position was seemingly inherited. The latest mayor, newly elected after his father, Scooter Burt, had retired, was the fifth Burt in office. He was nice enough, but maybe it was time to change things. Zach could charm anyone and would run a successful campaign. Although, Elise might be better suited to the role.

"You did a good job back there building Soupy. Nice work on the details. Are you ready to throw out candy from the passenger side as I drive?" Zach asked.

"No, I was going to be on the float, smiling and waving," Seth said.

"I don't think that's a good idea."

"Why not?" Seth turned toward his friend. Wasn't that exactly what everyone did in a parade? He wanted to be on the float, a visual reminder of his association with Soupy and vice versa. Besides the cameras, he wanted to catch the eye of those in the crowd who might see something and know who to tell.

"Seems dangerous," Zach muttered. He pulled the truck into the turn for the boardwalk and parked, idling the engine. "The flatbed doesn't have seatbelts."

"That's okay. You'll be driving slow. And I don't want to miss all the action." Seth unbuckled and got out of the truck. He'd never thought of his best friend as safety-conscious. Maybe he didn't want to be alone in the cab for the duration of the parade? Seth wished Zach would say that or be honest about whatever was bothering him.

Zach could be moody, especially if he'd fought with Mary. It was probably one of those off days. Seth wouldn't let his friend's sourness spoil his day. He strode around the bumper, almost tripping over his feet.

Soupy was the third vehicle and the first float of the parade. The truck parked at a slight incline where the sawmill's driveway met the road.

Seth strolled past the Lewises in the vehicle ahead. Their SUV was decked out in white and pink with a faux shingle roof, mimicking the inn's. He hadn't had a chance to chat with Ashley about her interview. Elise had promised to attend the filming. He could ask her. First, he had to find her.

He waved at the mayor in the back of his convertible with his wife at the wheel and continued to the start of the boardwalk. The giant cement planters used to prevent vehicles from driving on the pedestrian pathway had been moved in preparation for the event.

It was strange to have such unfettered access to the space. Seth felt exposed somehow. Like anything could happen.

The only safety guard between the boardwalk and the lake was a fairly flimsy railing about three feet tall. The boardwalk ended at a sidewalk that sloped toward the water before the mill. The spot provided access for small watercraft. He'd used it plenty of times to launch his old fishing boat.

With no barriers, the spot was vulnerable. Why was he even worried? Elise would have planned for every eventuality. Nothing would go wrong at one of her events.

"Hey, Seth," Elise called.

He glanced up and spotted her at the start of the boardwalk. He jogged the rest of the way to join her.

She held a clipboard to her chest. The look wasn't unusual. She often carried a checklist on the job. Today, she seemed on edge, more tightly wound than normal. He supposed the nervous energy she exuded was to be expected. First-time event. Cameras in position along the route. Eager visitors waiting. The stakes were high.

"Hey. The parade looks great," he greeted.

"Thanks, everyone really chipped in."

Her voice sounded wistful, far-off, distant. She didn't meet his gaze.

"Did you see Soupy?" He pointed to the mosasaurus behind the pickup.

She lifted her gaze to his and followed his direction. "Wow."

Her slightly breathless, single-word response wasn't quite as much as he'd been hoping for. But he'd take it all the same. "Construction wasn't easy. I watched a lot of online tutorials to learn how to shape the metal chicken wire frame underneath before building with wet newspaper strips and cardboard boxes."

"I can see you put a lot of hard work into it." She sniffed and pressed her lips together. Her skin was flushed, and her eyes were glassy.

If he didn't know any better, he'd think she was on the verge of tears. But he did know her. Elise never broke down, especially not in public. She needed a friend. "What's going on?" he murmured. "Are you alright?"

"Nothing..." She sighed and then stiffened her shoulders and grimaced. "Ugh. I'm a bad cliché. Sorry."

"It's okay. You can talk to me. Openly. Honestly."

"Can I? I'm supposed to be your manager. I shield you."

Now he turned to stone. What did she have to say? No, he trusted her. If she needed support, she could lean on him. "If we aren't truthful with each other, what kind of friendship do we have?" He reached a hand to lightly touch her shoulder.

"Okay. The other day at the lighthouse, I didn't like how the interview went." She scrunched her nose.

"How did it go?" He dropped his hand, breaking the physical contact.

"Like you'd expect," she muttered.

That wasn't a real answer. He'd have to pull the response out of her. "Really? Ashley has so much charisma and loves the limelight. I figured she'd become the scene-stealing star of the project."

Elise widened her eyes and gaped. "You did?"

He shrugged. "Well... yeah. Was I wrong?"

Elise shook her head.

"So what's the issue?"

"She just... went off on a tangent about her ghost. Pete kept at her with a ton of questions. I'm worried she'll steal the focus. And how did Pete seem to know about Ashley's *haunted lighthouse*?" Elise made air quotes.

Seth chuckled. "Maybe the interview will heighten the paranormal experiences others have had on the water. I'm the only Soupy eyewitness. They'll need to make sense of every story they can to help illuminate how a monster could live here."

"I suppose..."

"And if they found old copies of *Loon Lake Life* from last summer, they might have read Zach's op-ed about Ashley's ghost encounter. Don't worry. I wouldn't mind sharing the attention, as long as the search finds answers about Soupy. Focus on this." Seth held his hands wide. "Your big event."

"Elise?" Tim called from the front car. "Do you have a minute before we start?"

"I'd better go."

"Do you feel better?" Seth asked.

She met his gaze and slowly nodded. "I do. Thanks."

He reached for her hand and squeezed. "Don't let me keep you. I'd better line up. Don't want to cause a delay and throw the whole event into chaos."

She smiled, slipped her fingers out of his grasp, and strode toward the mayor's convertible.

He wasn't worried about Ashley stealing the spotlight. He had his path, and she had hers. The only woman he focused any energy on was Elise. For a second, he'd proved himself capable of being someone she could turn to and unload a burden on. He'd be that and so much more.

Finding Soupy was the start to making his mark and being worthy of her. He wouldn't miss his shot.

* * *

*That went surprisingly well...*

As Elise followed her summons and headed to the mayor's convertible, she absorbed Seth's response. Since the interview, she'd spent a lot of time worrying, replaying what had happened on camera and how she could downplay the impact of Ashley's statements. Almost every sentence had been worthy of a viral soundbite. Elise cringed again. An editor would have a field day making a salacious teaser from the answers.

More than her ongoing disdain for Ashley's ability to turn every situation into a chance for herself to shine in the spotlight, Elise had been nervous about what and how much to share with Seth. Because the interview questions highlighted the crew's shrewd research, and Elise looked like an amateur by not anticipating them. She didn't want Seth to think she'd been unprepared and caught off guard. She had. But she wanted to continue to exude her typical reserved confidence, the attitude she'd become known for. If she wasn't capable in her role as his manager, she worried he'd cut her loose. She liked spending time with him under the guise of handling things.

And yet, sharing her concerns with him, he'd lightened her burden. In fact, he'd taken it off her shoulders and tossed it in the lake where it sank like a stone.

She could count on him. His reasonableness was a wonderful discovery. What else was he hiding behind the handsome façade and kind manners?

"Elise, hey," Tim called as she neared.

"Good afternoon, Mr. Mayor. Mrs. Mayor." She nodded at Amanda behind the wheel.

Per usual, Amanda rolled her eyes. She hated formal address.

Elise insisted on it. Being the mayor's wife wasn't so easy. Appearances had to be maintained at all times. In a small town, everyone talked.

"Can you believe Lonnie tried to take over as grand marshal of the parade?" Tim asked, adding a guffaw and staring pointedly at the line of cars behind him. "My dad warned me. Lonnie had been eyeing the mayoral position for decades and tried to get Dad's endorsement before the recent election."

Elise had no reaction. Of course she could have predicted that. Ashley wasn't the only person in town looking for a little attention. Lonnie's failed bid for mayor wouldn't stop him from seeking the limelight, no matter how small the chance at celebrity. She followed the mayor's gaze and spotted Lonnie several vehicles back. He rode in the bed of a pickup truck surrounded by mountains of candy, winning the hearts of the voters through their stomachs.

"How is the production going? Do you need anything from me or my office?" Tim asked.

She turned to Tim and shook her head. "So far, so good. Seth has been interviewed, and so has Ashley. The cameras have been rolling on the lake. I think they were pleased with the footage from the fun run." She was glad the forms had been discovered and that she hadn't wasted the crew's time.. At least today, with the focus on the parade floats and the community members who had all already submitted their documentation—except for Mr. Willie at the inn—should be an easy day.

"Has our elusive, infamous monster made an appearance?" Tim asked, wiggling his eyebrows.

"Nothing to report yet."

"Good, good. And everything is ready?"

"The crew is stationed to film the parade. More b-roll probably." She pointed to a camera at the start of the raised boardwalk.

"We should probably get started soon. Good work on organizing today. Are you sure you don't need anything from me?"

She knew he wanted to help. But she hated the sensation he was prodding for something, some outcome or offer she couldn't guess at. His question was innocuous and the sort of typical offer anyone in a position of power would make without assuming it would be accepted. She heard an edge in his words like a warning.

She must be wrong. Tim wouldn't play games. He'd directly tell her to stop doing something or to back off. What else could linger under the ask? "Are you asking to be on camera?"

Amanda chortled.

"Do you want to be interviewed?" Elise persisted. "I'm sure I can add you to the list."

"Oh, definitely not," Tim said in a second without a pause. "But if you need me, I'm here. We all are. The success of these events and the documentary, or whatever it turns into, will capture a picture of our town. We will all be impacted by what develops. Don't feel like you can't ask for help or that you have no one to turn to. Because I assure you, I care."

Elise nodded, tears stinging her eyes. She struggled because, for so many years, no one stepped up. It was assumed she would do the work. Starting with group projects in middle school, she put her head down and did the labor without complaint. It was effective to be her own boss. She was often lonely.

A whistle cut through the air.

Elise lifted her gaze to spot Kate standing with a camera at the start of the raised boardwalk.

Kate motioned with her arm to hurry up.

Why? Did the producer once again have some knowledge that alluded Elise? She hated the hair-raising sensation on her arms. "Okay, let's get started."

Elise stepped back as Amanda turned up the patriotic music on her car radio and slowly pulled onto the boardwalk.

Cheers erupted.

One by one, the vehicles disengaged their brakes and rolled forward.

Behind the Burts, the Lewises, the Soupy float, the sheriff's department, and the nearby fire brigade assembled. The parade would be loud, with lights already flashing and the sirens primed and ready to blare. But at least there would be candy.

Seth walked alongside the Soupy float, carrying a plastic bag full of stickers and candy. The slow pace promised him plenty of time to meet and greet the eager audience.

Or that would have been the plan.

But in slow motion, disaster struck.

As Zach's truck rolled down the sawmill's dock and navigated onto the boardwalk, the flatbed holding Soupy broke free.

The monster of Loon Lake slid into the dark water. The gray paper-mache and cardboard beast bobbed up and down.

Seth stood near the shore, hands over his face. He turned and met her gaze with a look of pure confusion.

"Got it," Kate said, her voice crisp and clear among the echoes of cries and shocked gasps.

So much for being in control. Her last item before focusing on the documentary had gone awry. At least she didn't need to worry about messing anything else up. What was Elise even doing? He didn't deserve infamy. If she couldn't manage simple tasks, what could she offer to Seth? Nothing.

Elise ran to him, not caring if she was making a scene on camera or not. "Seth, I'm sorry." She leaned close, whispering into his ear. "I should have triple-checked the connections on every vehicle." She'd trusted others with a job. She knew she couldn't do that. The only way to be sure everything was handled properly was to take care of all the work herself.

He pulled his hands away from his face and offered her a sad smile. "You have nothing to apologize for. Accidents happen. And it made good TV. Look." He lifted his chin.

Elise turned, slowly taking in the action around them.

Soupy hadn't fully submerged. His open jaw protruded from the surface. As the forward vehicles in the parade continued, seemingly unaware of the chaos unfolding behind them, the boardwalk cleared.

Visitors swarmed to the railing, pointing and chattering. A few flashes of light followed. Laughter rose above the cacophony.

Sure, the float livened up the parade. But she'd do anything to absorb the cost and not make more of a sideshow of Seth's documentary. "This is all my fault. Honestly, I can't apologize enough."

"Hey." He stroked her arm with a finger.

Her skin sizzled along the point of contact, and she turned to face him. The tender expression in his eyes twisted her heart. She shut her eyes and shook her head. She couldn't bear to face him.

A warm palm covered her hand.

She snapped open her gaze.

He reached for her hand and squeezed her fingers. "You can't be in charge of everything. You have to trust others. Maybe not Zach…"

Despite herself, Elise giggled. "Definitely not Zach." She huffed.

"Let me give him a hand to get this mess cleaned up." He squeezed her hands once more before pulling away. "Don't worry. It'll be alright."

She almost believed him. Seth made everything better. His good heart came through in every worst-case scenario. She trusted him. "I'm supposed to be managing things for you. I'm letting you down."

"Never." He strode towards the idling pickup.

She scanned the crowd again, relieved to see the cameras focused on the tourists and not capturing the interlude between her and Seth. At least she'd finished her final special event. She could devote her attention to handling the rest of filming for Seth and make things as smooth—and normal—as possible.

# Chapter Nine

A few days later, Seth was seated behind the log cabin museum with one of the best views of the lake. He liked how the green of the Aspens and Pines popped under an overcast sky. Chairs and lights had been set up for his next interview. After filming so many community events, he found himself even more relaxed than usual for the latest round of conversational back and forth with Pete.

And as far as he was concerned, he couldn't have asked for better weather. Soupy didn't like sunshine or bright skies. The creature had been spotted a on dark, cloudy day in winter, with two other sightings in spring and summer while under a threat for severe thunderstorms.

With any luck, the interview would finish on time so he could lead an impromptu tour. Or—better yet—convince Grant to take him out on the water to hunt.

Pete and Kate had not discussed any boat tours of the lake yet.

Seth knew they had begun to collect samples of the freshwater. He had spotted them a few times. But they hadn't asked him to participate. Seth was beginning to find the whole process a little underwhelming.

He was kept to the side. He knew he didn't have much to offer the scientists, but he still wanted to be involved. At least he could count on Elise to watch out for him.

She stood near the back of the log cabin, chatting with the camera operator and other crew. She gestured with her arms, probably indicating electrical outlets.

Seth was glad she had allowed filming here. The log cabin had become one of his favorite spots and not just because she was always here. Or not totally.

She crossed the grass toward him with the sound tech. "Good morning."

"Hi," he said, his voice breathless. "Thanks for letting us do this."

She waved off the thanks. "The museum is closed today, so it's perfect timing."

The sound tech clipped a small microphone to the collar of Seth's Search for Soupy polo. The shirt had been Elise's idea, to present his brand in a professional way on camera. In all things, she was right.

"Are you ready?" she asked as the sound tech finished and walked away.

"I am." He smiled.

She didn't return the expression. Her face clouded, and her eyes darted from side to side.

"What's wrong?"

"Maybe nothing. I keep replaying Ashley's interview from the other day."

"Oh?" he asked. Elise had mentioned it at the parade. Had something else happened? He hated that she troubled herself on his behalf. But he was also a little pleased to have so much of her focus on his project that she worried about details.

Elise bit her lip.

"Bad?" He was perplexed. Ashley was always so cheerful and energetic. How could she have done anything less than her best?

"I keep thinking about how she manipulated the interview to focus on her ghost."

He nodded. He'd expected Ashley would.

"A lot about her ghost."

"That's okay. She probably needed to tell someone. Good for her." When Ashley had first mentioned a ghost, she hadn't explained every encounter. She hadn't had anyone supporting her. But something must have happened because Christopher completely believed it, too. He wouldn't encourage her just because he loved her. He was a skeptic. It had taken Seth years to get Christopher to understand and acknowledge Soupy. But then he had become one of the monster's staunchest defenders. "Don't worry about it. No one else has had an up-close encounter. They can only share their experiences. And maybe the TV crew will find a link between everything."

Elise wrinkled her brow. "Between that and my parade mess-up, I'm worried the focus is shifting. This is your big project. You deserve the spotlight." She set her mouth in a hard line, and the muscles in her jaw twitched. She remained unconvinced. Seth didn't know how to reassure her.

Pete approached and sat in the other chair. "Good morning. Shall we get started?"

Elise nodded and backed away.

Seth wanted to tell her to stay. Not to go. But he couldn't. "I'm ready."

The cameraman counted down from five.

"Seth, you have mentioned three encounters with Soupy," Pete said.

"That's correct."

"Once you saw the beast's mouth and eye, and twice its flippers."

Seth nodded.

"I'd like to go back to that first encounter. Because it seems to have been the most momentous."

"Seeing a giant mouth of pointy teeth does leave an impact on a person."

Pete chuckled. "I should think so. Start wherever you wish and tell us what you want us to know about that encounter."

Seth blew out a sigh. "It was a frigid winter day. The sort of dry, bitter cold that you can't shake out of your bones. It was a Saturday. I was up early watching cartoons. I liked to sneak downstairs and pour myself a bowl of cereal without waking my parents. For as long as they slept, I could do whatever I wanted."

"Helicopter parents?"

Seth shook his head. "Not back then. It's just... I was never lonely growing up because I was never alone." He and Zach had been best friends since kindergarten. His mom and dad wanted to be with him and his little sister around the clock. With so many big personalities around him, Seth felt overshadowed and followed in their wake rather than ever charting his own path. "But Saturday mornings were my quiet time. My sister would sleep in, too. I turned on cartoons and zoned out. Did a lot of thinking."

"So you are watching TV?" Pete prodded.

"Right, yes, and my dad turned off the TV. He'd set an alarm and told me to get my gear on because we'd be ice fishing all day. I hated ice fishing. It was boring, but I knew complaining wouldn't get me out of it.

On weekends, I had three choices. Watching my little sister play ice hockey, spending the day on chores, or ice fishing."

"And you picked the lesser of the evils?"

Seth shrugged. "I could tell it was different. He never woke up specifically to go anywhere with me. So I got changed and stuffed my backpack with all the books I'd been reading. We trudged through the snowbanks to a designated spot on the ice. Back in those days, the town used to set up civic ice fishing huts that anyone could reserve."

Pete shuddered. "I can't imagine it. I don't think I want to." He laughed again.

"On this particular day, we had been inside the hut for about two hours. Catching nothing. I was reading a book about dinosaurs. My dad had stepped out to get us hot chocolate from the stand nearby. From the corner of my eye, I saw something through the hole in the ice. Something dark. A shiver went down my whole body. I put the book down and laid on the ice, brushing the snow into the hole. And then it moved again and blinked, its jaw opened. Thankfully, it was too large to get its mouth into the hole, or I would have been swallowed whole."

"That's terrifying. What did you do? Did you run for help?"

"I was completely frozen in shock. And as I realized it couldn't get me, I stared at it and memorized every detail. The point of its teeth. The way the eyelid covered the eyeball. It seemed like we were locked in a staring contest for hours. But really it was probably a minute. Dad came back, and it swam off, diving deep, a little water splashing out of the hole as it swam away."

"And what did you tell your dad?"

"Nothing right away. I sat up, drank my cocoa, and tried to warm myself up. Then I remembered I had seen the creature before. I found the page in my book and showed my dad."

"And what did he say?"

"Nothing to start. He didn't discourage me or say I was wrong. We went home, and I started researching what I could have seen. I had plenty of time to devote hours to the library because I didn't play sports like my dad. I don't think he knew how to relate to me. We were so different.

When I asked to go ice fishing again, I shocked him in the best way. The next visit was the start of a long five-year period without a sighting. Dad didn't just encourage me. He joined me in my research. We spent hours together, reading and learning. When I'd go into the store with him, I'd work and tell him what I learned. We began mapping the lake and studying everything we could. Soupy became the core of our bond. We took trips to museums all over the country to learn as much as we could. We spent countless hours together. By the end of his life, though, Dad was a bigger believer than me."

"Is this search about keeping his memory alive?"

Seth shook his head. "I don't need to. I'll never forget him. This search is about resolution. What started as a journey of one has become a town-wide endeavor. And no one else has ever seen him. I am the luckiest person on earth because I have the best friends on this planet. I want to do right by everyone. And I know we will. I know we will find Soupy."

* * *

Elise swiped at her lower lashes and sniffed. She'd heard the story in bits and pieces over the years. But had never listened as Seth explain what Soupy meant.

The monster wasn't only a diversion. The creature had brought together a father and a son in a way nothing else had or could. Was he moving forward with the investigation to honor his dad?

Elise had thought Seth wanted some sort of validation. Which didn't fit with what she knew of him. Seth's effervescent sweetness and joy radiated off him, brightening the lives of those around him. He didn't seek outside opinions or ask for help with his choices. She didn't quite get his motivation for this project, and that had made her nervous.

Today, however, everything became clear, and she had a better footing. Seeking to cement his father's memory made much more sense. Seth wouldn't do something for himself alone.

"What will you do after the search is over?" Pete asked.

Seth shrugged. "You seem very optimistic that you'll find Soupy."

"Aren't you?"

"I am hopeful. But the channel and access to Lake Superior is a contributing factor in how hard it has been to gather evidence to date."

"Are you saying it's a long shot?"

Seth shook his head and crossed his arms over his chest. He had his serious face. "Whatever happens, the lake and its creatures need protection. We aren't immune to modern environmental concerns."

Elise was heartened to hear him say he thought it would be difficult to get definitive proof. She didn't want him discouraged when the search came up empty. She admired his dedication to preserving the habitat for all.

"Do you think you saw a Mosasaurus in the lake all those years ago?" Pete asked.

Seth nodded. "I do. I've tried to find any other creature that it could be. Trust me. It would be a lot easier to claim I saw a shark or an alligator." He shrugged. "I know both sound outlandish, but people know those animals. A mosasaurus might as well be a dragon."

"What's stopping you from identifying the creature as something already known in the zoological community?" Pete asked.

"I can't shake what I saw or what I felt. When you have an extraordinary encounter, you can't forget or downplay what happened. That's dishonest. The teeth were terrible and awesome. The memory burned into my brain. I would love to get definitive proof, but I don't want the animal captured. As you've said, the beast is not a menace."

"Just a missing link?"

"Exactly. What else remains out there in the wild?"

She felt better after hearing him say the words. His friends didn't understand how or why, but supported him regardless. Because at the end of the day, what was Seth guilty of besides telling himself a story to reframe his world in a way he could process? She did the same, didn't she?

"CUT," the camera operator called.

"Seth, great stuff today. Thanks," Pete said.

"Thank you," Seth said.

Elise smiled as she neared.

"And thanks for giving us access here, Elise. Perfect backdrop for us," Pete added with a smile that didn't reach his eyes.

She nodded. "Of course."

"I'm heading back to LA for a week. Kate and I have meetings scheduled for other projects. Always have to hustle in showbusiness." Pete laughed.

Elise didn't share his mirth. "What about the other interviews? You're meeting with Molly tomorrow."

Pete shook his head. "I've rescheduled. But don't worry. We aren't abandoning you. The research crew will stay. We'll give you all a break from the cameras for a little bit. When we get back, we'll have a tour on the lake," Pete said.

Elise nearly sighed with relief. A week without having to worry about getting caught on tape? Thank you, yes, please. "Sounds good."

"I'm pleased with what we have so far." Pete clapped Seth on the shoulder. "It's all thanks to you. You're the heart of this project."

Seth blushed.

Elise relaxed. She agreed. And thank goodness for it. Seth was the heart and soul of the project. And Ashley couldn't distract from that. "We'll see you when you get back."

Seth unclipped his microphone and set it on the chair.

Pete walked away.

Seth exhaled a heavy breath. "Was I okay?"

"Better than okay. You're a natural. You did great." She wanted to rub his arm in encouragement. But she didn't dare give in to the urge. "A little time off from the cameras to live our real lives will be nice."

"I'm anxious about the boat tour."

"Do you want me to talk to Grant?"

Seth shook his head. "I just don't want to disappoint anyone."

This time, she did reach for his hand and squeeze. She felt that too, so deeply. What was all her hard work for if not to assist everyone else? What was community if not pulling together?

"Do you want to get dinner? Tomorrow? Just the two of us?" Seth's voice cracked.

Her toes curled in her shoes. "Like a date?" She wasn't sure if she had asked the question or merely gasped the words, struggling for breath.

He nodded. The corner of his mouth lifting in a tilted smile.

She knew that look. The self-deprecating grin like he readied himself to accept her dismissal and brush off her negative response like it wasn't a big deal.

But he was brave for asking the question she'd been circling in her own head.

"Yes, I do." She squeezed his hand once more. Yes, she really, really did. He stroked his thumb over her palm, sending a jolt of awareness along every nerve ending.

In her pocket, her phone buzzed. She reluctantly dropped her hand from his grip to retrieve the device.

**Tim Burt:** *Stop by when you get a chance.*

"Everything okay?" Seth asked.

She shuddered. "I might be on my way to a public reprimand. Tim wants to see me." She typed a quick reply. **OMW.**

"Remember, he's not your boss. The parade took a turn, but it recovered," Seth added.

His kindness poured salt into her open wound. "Sure," she agreed, eager to move on and face the mayor. "I need to get a larger pot for the sapling I'm growing. I have to go to the hardware store. I might as well head there now. It'll be fine."

"Mrs. Fitz-Ash? She's growing? That's so good to hear."

And once again, he soothed her with his genuine caring. Who else would remember the name of a plant? "Bye," she said. "See you tomorrow."

"Looking forward to it," he replied.

She left while she could. The warmth of his smile tempted her to forgo everything else for the pleasure of his company.

She wasn't one to shirk her responsibilities. During the short drive, as soon as she started the car until she parked at the strip mall, she prepared for the deserved roasting.

Seth was right. The parade had continued after the sinking.

Following a delay, as it was determined the trailer would be fished out of the lake after the vehicles were all out of the way, Zach had driven the truck along the route. Seth walked alongside. If a tourist hadn't heard of Soupy before the incident, the uninformed quickly learned about Loon Lake's legend in the aftermath.

Elise had worried others might have a similar soggy fate. She stood guard at the lake's public access ramp. No other float softened the indignity of sinking. She'd been most apprehensive about Lonnie's towering taffy float. But his trailer hadn't wobbled.

If she were a conspiracy theorist, she'd spot sabotage.

Why? To make Seth look foolish? Everyone in town loved him. The TV crew adored him, too. More likely than not, she'd be the target. And she didn't have time or energy to live in a state of paranoia.

She pushed through the door at the hardware store.

"That was fast," Tim greeted behind the counter. "I didn't mean for you to drop everything and race over here."

Elise shrugged and strolled inside, scanning the pots on the ground. She was glad for her convenient excuse to avoid his gaze. "I need a larger pot for a plant. Seemed like a good time to get that checked off my to-do list."

She bent and picked up a large blue pot. The molded plastic resembled painted terracotta. Luckily for her, the pot was neither as heavy nor as expansive as a ceramic piece.

She set the pot on the counter and handed him cash.

He extended the receipt. "Okay. Now that that's done. Let's chat."

His serious tone and direct stare sent a shiver along her spine. In all of the chaos, she'd forgotten that she'd hurt him, too. She'd been in charge of a moment in town history that would be remembered as embarrassing, but he would be remembered as the mayor. "I'm so sorry about the parade."

"Don't be. We recovered, and everyone loved it. I don't want to go backwards. I am interested in looking forward. And I'm serious that I want to be included and help."

He wasn't quite scolding her. His words held a sharp edge. Like he'd reached the limit of his patience. She'd always imagined he couldn't be pushed.

"To that end," he said with deliberation, "I'd very much like to be hands-on with your next event. In fact, I'm going to insist on it."

"Oh, well..." She pressed her tongue to the roof of her mouth, stalling. Now she felt worse. She'd clearly misled him. "I don't have anything else planned."

"No?" He frowned. "I figured you'd have a glitzy, red carpet premiere planned for Seth."

"Definitely. That's at least a year away." She was glad to shift the focus where it should be. With her events behind her and fundraising still months away, she could give Seth her full attention. "Good idea. I'd be glad for help."

"Great. I know you'll want to do something big."

"I will?"

"For Seth? Of course. The two of you are a nice pair."

She blushed. She wanted to ask him in what way, as much as she longed to pretend this conversation had never happened.

"I also know," Tim said smoothly, cutting through her thoughts like a knife in butter, "how hard you are working. Your efforts are seen and appreciated."

She swallowed the lump bobbing in her throat. "Anyone would do the same."

"No, they wouldn't. You have always done your best for this town and without seeking praise. But I want to heap it on you anyway. You are valued and important. You have my gratitude."

His tone was sincere but sharp. She didn't know why, but she couldn't stop thinking every vowel cut a little deeper. Had the mayor praised her or warned her? She wasn't sure. She was letting her insecurities rule her.

Her motivation to do her best by the town might be trivial to others. It guided her. She smiled and grabbed the pot off the counter. "Thanks, Tim. See you later."

And she strode out of the room. Because she wouldn't worry about what other people thought. She had to live her life. With a tiny smidge of courage, she'd make her own happiness.

Just like Seth.

# Chapter Ten

Tomorrow was finally today. Seth stood at the boardwalk railing, staring across the lake. Since he'd asked her out, he hadn't stopped counting the seconds or pinching his arm. This was real life and he was thrilled. The only thing that could make his unbelievable day any better was if Soupy appeared right now.

Seth held his breath and shut his eyes. He'd made countless vision boards and repeated mantras on and off for years, working the law of attraction to realize his biggest goal. But so far, he hadn't willed the monster out of its hiding place. Seth squinted through one eye and released a heavy exhale. Nothing. The TV crew would get answers, he was sure.

He studied the gentle ripples on the dark water, noting nothing amiss. Too bad the Soupy parade float had been fished out of the water. He'd had an idea to keep the cardboard and paper-mache statue—or better, get a waterproof replacement —as a photo opportunity for tourists. While he hadn't had enough time to craft the best Soupy replica possible, he'd found the submerged monster, only its jaws visible from the surface, charming and mysterious. Its presence changed the landscape for the better.

With the summer days stretching well into summer nights, he loved spending every opportunity outside. Including—and most especially—while waiting on his date.

Yesterday, in the thrill of the moment, he had asked Elise out. Riding high after the interview and the chance to be honest with his fears about the investigation, he surged ahead. Only after the fact did he realize the problem.

Where could he take her?

The nicest restaurant in town was the inn. Was that too much for a first date? The old train station turned microbrewery and grill quickly filled up with tourists. The boardwalk boasted more fast, casual dining. He loved the pizza at By the Slice, as well as the fries and burgers at the pub. Would she want something better?

He could have cooked. He was decent with a grill and would offer a more impressive meal during the summer than the winter. But then they'd be at his house. Would that be too intimate? If he asked one of his other friends for help, he knew they would have agreed, but then he'd have invited everyone else into their business, and he didn't really want that either.

He glanced at the lake once again. Anything could happen on a warm summer evening. Maybe even the impossible.

"Hey," Elise called.

He turned and smiled. She was wearing jeans and heels, and her hair was down. She'd made an effort. Was his collar shirt enough to show he'd done the same? "Hi," he squeaked. He coughed. "You look nice."

"Thanks." She tucked a strand of hair behind her ear. "You do, too." A soft pink blush colored her cheeks.

She looked pretty and unguarded, so different from her usual polished persona. He hadn't seen her without a bun since middle school. Her thick hair hung over her shoulders like brown silk. How many people had she shown this version of herself? He was glad to be among the limited number, even if he was a little jealous imagining other men having the same opportunity.

"So," she rubbed her palms together. "Where are we headed?"

"Your choice." He extended both arms. "The boardwalk is all yours."

"You didn't make any plans?" she asked.

Her words had a hesitant edge. "Hard to make reservations at businesses that don't believe in them." He chuckled.

She softened her tight smile. "Good point. Only the inn takes those and..."

"Say no more." He'd never quite understood why she and Ashley rubbed each other the wrong way. But he was aware enough not to put her in an uncomfortable spot this evening. "Wherever you want to go, I'll follow."

She tapped a finger to her chin. "Are you sure?"

"Completely."

"Because what if I do something unexpected?"

Like lean in for a kiss? He was hoping for it. He swallowed. "I'm sure I'm up for the challenge. As long as it's not laser tag."

Her eyes widened, and she shook her head. "Never that."

He crossed his heart. "On my honor."

"Ice cream for dinner?" she continued after a beat.

"Oh." He snapped back. "We can try. If Zach hasn't sold out for the day." He was surprised. He didn't think she'd want Zach involved in their first date. Or any date. Not that she knew his best friend was his self-declared dating coach. Maybe this was better. Maybe this was fate. Zach could help steer him onto the right path if he started veering off. "After you."

She gripped her hands in front of her and strolled forward.

He joined her, regretting her closed-off body language. He

couldn't try to reach for her hand or brush her arm without being obvious.

"I didn't realize how nice it would feel to have the cameras gone," she said after they'd fallen into too long of a silence. "I feel like I can breathe again."

He hadn't felt tension in the pause. With her, he was always comfortable and excited, like he was curled up in his bed on Christmas Eve. "I hadn't really noticed a change either way."

"Really? Gosh, you're the focus of attention. I'd think you'd be even more aware of how the crew follows your every move."

He shrugged. "I forget the cameras are there, to be honest. I'm glad for the chance to speak so openly and honestly about what I've seen and experienced."

"Everyone wants to be heard." She reached for his bicep and squeezed.

They reached Scoops, There It Is. He stepped forward and held the door open. He could manage at least one small act of chivalry.

She brushed past him and entered, resting her hand on his elbow for a second.

He might as well have been branded. His skin scalded at the featherlight touch. She had marked him. Forever.

"Yo!" Zach called out, abbreviating his typical nineties-themed sales pitch. "Seth and Elise. Hey. What brings you two in? Need me to get ready for my close-up?"

Dressed in his white overalls and highlighter-yellow shirt, Zach was hard to miss. In Seth's opinion, his best friend didn't need the bright costume to stand out. Fiercely loyal and devoted to doing his best, the gregarious Zach was either a love him or hate him figure. Although, Seth didn't know what Elise thought.

"That is a shame," Elise said.

Oops. Seth had zoned out during the conversation. "Sorry? What did I miss?"

"Out of rocky road and mint chip. I have the basics left today," Zach said.

"I'm good with the classics," Elise said.

"Me too," Seth smiled.

"What brings you two to my little shop if you're not here to interrogate me before my interview?" Zach asked, grabbing a dish and scooping out ice cream.

"The cameras are gone for a week. Were you scheduled soon?" Seth asked.

"No, nothing yet." Zach set one dish on the counter and scooped up the next. "I want to apologize again for what happened at the parade. I guess I didn't check everything as thoroughly as I thought. I'm sorry."

"Thanks," Elise murmured.

Seth knew by her stiff posture that she didn't fully believe Zach's sincerity. But she didn't know everything about Zach. Or his distractions. "We'll be sure to give you a heads up before the crew stops by."

"If you aren't here to prep me, did you stop by with the latest issue of *Loon Lake Life*? I didn't see any boxes today."

Seth gaped and stared at Elise.

"What's wrong?" she asked.

"I forgot I had to print this week's issue. I have it all set. I just have to run the job, collate, assemble, and drop off the copies," he said.

"Is that a lot of work?" she asked.

He nodded.

"Can I help?" she asked.

"Would you?" Seth asked. Her help would make the work infinitely more enjoyable.

"Sure, why not? Unless..." she leaned close. "You have a laser tag meet-up planned instead." She smirked and chuckled.

"Never that," Seth promised. "Although, if I remember correctly from the senior class graduation party, you were doing quite well for our team."

"Until I tripped over my own two feet, twisted my ankle, and had to get carried out by Christopher. I think Ashley wanted to leave me in a heap on the floor. She was so mad."

*She wasn't the only one.* A surge of heat from the memory bubbled in his veins. When he'd spotted Elise in Christopher's arms, Seth had nearly attacked the other man to grab Elise himself. Instead, he'd frozen in place as Elise's gun misfired. "And then you accidentally hit my target and got me out, too. Just work tonight. No secret rendezvous. But your assistance would be hugely appreciated."

"And you'll owe me a raincheck for tonight?"

"Wait," Zach interrupted. "Are you two here on a date?"

Heat flared in Seth's cheeks.

Elise smiled at him, reaching for his arm and slipping her hand into the crook.

"Well, good for you. It's about time. I figured you two missed your opportunity and were forever friend-zoned," Zach said. He set the other dish of ice cream on the counter. "Hold on one sec." He flipped a series of switches on the wall, dimming the lights and lowering a disco ball.

Nineties R&B filled the room. The playlist wasn't that different from the usual songs played on repeat. The singer was more soulful and pleading. "I'll be in the back if you need me."

He disappeared behind the curtain leading to the back room and walk-in freezer.

Had Zach totally ruined Seth's chance with his mood-setting overkill? He met Elise's gaze.

And she laughed.

He grinned back. "Sorry."

"It's okay. Sort of inevitable, right? At least he's supportive," she said, reaching for her ice cream. "We'd better eat up and then head to your store. I bet we can get everything printed and delivered before ten tomorrow morning. Two more hands should help."

She had no idea. He was grateful for her in more ways than he could count. Maybe he'd get a chance to show her how special she was. Maybe—one day—he could be the one to rescue her.

* * *

Behind the wheel in her car, Elise tailed Seth. She wasn't surprised that their date had taken a turn. When she was with him, she was almost easygoing, able to set aside her plans and go with the flow. He put her at ease.

Elise knew what to expect with Seth. Liking a man she'd known for so long meant understanding him. She didn't get offended by the offhand way he had asked her out. As soon as he'd issued the invitation, she knew it was completely spontaneous. And, as she had dressed with care for herself more than anything, she was fully prepared for him to forget to make reservations anywhere. Wearing jeans, her favorite cardigan, and wedge heels, she'd made an effort but wouldn't be out of place or uncomfortable if Seth presented her with a picnic basket dinner. But she hoped for something better than sitting on the grass.

Not that she was looking for a fancy night out. In their town, only one restaurant boasted a wine list, and Elise wasn't exactly eager to let the Lewises know about her personal life. The only option left was the boardwalk, which wasn't a fit for anonymity. But she'd rather face the comments head-on than hear about it later. So when Seth had asked what she wanted to eat, she hadn't paused. She'd said ice cream and headed into the headquarters of the town's biggest gossip.

She knew Zach was Seth's best friend and would learn all about the situation from Seth. Rather than let Seth relay the information and have Zach question her behavior after the fact, she preferred to show her genuine feelings for Seth. Zach would all too gladly rally the well-meaning citizens to threaten her if she hurt Seth. For good reason, Seth was the town's favorite son. The kindest person around, he might be the only one without an oversized ego.

But Elise had another motive for her choice, too. She wanted to see what sort of response she'd get from Zach after the parade incident. His apology seemed genuine but guarded, like he wasn't entirely truthful about the accident. For Seth's sake, she dropped it. But she wouldn't forget.

At the printshop, she parked and grabbed her purse, pulling out a ponytail holder and making a messy bun with her perfectly straightened tresses. She hated to waste the style but couldn't stand having loose hair when working. She shot a glance at the end of the strip mall.

The hardware store was closed.

She exhaled a heavy sigh. Tim had offered his support again, and she felt small. She knew her response was ridiculous. The mayor was supportive and had always treated her like a partner instead of an employee. Still, she hated that she'd embarrassed the town on film.

"Everything okay?" Seth asked. "Do you see something?"

She shook her head. "Everything's fine. I was just... thinking."

"I'm sorry I ruined our night," he said in a rush.

She reached a hand to his elbow, lightly grazing him. "It's okay. Accidents happen. I should be apologizing to you for the parade."

"Why? I had a great time."

"But all of your hard work sank into the lake," she protested.

"Or maybe Soupy found home." Seth unlocked the front door and flipped on the lights.

She blinked. Going from soft twilight to overhead fluorescents was jarring.

"I have everything formatted and saved," Seth said, heading to the counter and powering on his computer.

"Do you want any proofreads before you start printing?"

"Well, you can read it while I warm up the printers and load the rolls. It can take a while. We only use a tabloid size to cut down on costs and time. I need to head into the back to start up everything."

"Sure. Don't let me get in the way." He inched his hand close to hers on the counter.

Standing near, she sniffed his cedar aftershave and felt the warmth rolling off his skin. She felt safe and welcome. She didn't dare reach for his hand with hers but was close enough to imagine it, a delicious torture.

"You're never in the way," he murmured.

She nibbled her lip, all too aware of him.

"And hey, thanks for helping me."

She smiled. He was the best person she knew. "It's my pleasure."

He covered her hand. "About what Zach said."

She darted her tongue over her dry lower lip. "The friend zone thing?"

He nodded, staring at her mouth.

"Why do we have to label anything?" She raised a shaky hand to brush a loose strand of hair behind her right ear. Her voice trembled. "And what's with a timeline? I didn't know there was a doomsday clock on dating."

He swallowed, his Adam's apple bobbing. "You're right. Like usual."

*But still...Zach sort of has a point.* She hated to give Zach any credit, but she understood at some point Seth would move on if nothing happened.

The air between Elise and Seth sizzled and charged. Every tiny hair lifted on her skin, from the nape of her neck down her arms. She curled her toes, waiting. Why not lean forward and kiss him now? Put them both out of their misery.

With her heartbeat thundering in her ears, she focused on his mouth. He parted his lips. She swallowed, tilting her chin up.

He stepped away, officially killing the mood. "Okay, the PDFs are here for you to view," he pointed to the icons on the screen. "I'll be in the back if you find anything. Although, maybe just write it all down first and then we can make the edits?"

"Sounds like a plan." She nodded, ignoring the sharp stab in her gut and the wave of regret threatening to pull her under.

Gritting her back teeth, she narrowed her gaze at the monitor. She absolutely would not press her hands to her flushed cheeks to cool her heated skin. Or run after him and smash her lips against his.

He'd decided against making out. Her rational mind understood how much work lay ahead of them. He probably wanted to get started. Nothing more. Nothing less.

And she had sent him mixed signals, too. She'd killed the mood. She'd learn from her mistake. Another day, she'd try again.

She waited until he disappeared before she started clicking the files. She was eager to give him the best help she could offer: her critical eye. But she knew her serious grimace while reviewing was off-putting. She didn't mind working on a date but would prefer not to make any faces at him.

The first two articles were the standard *Loon Lake Life* fodder. A top ten list of must-dos for tourists and a guest column from Lonnie about his perfect day.

What had started as a way for Zach to needle Christopher had morphed into a tourist trap with coupons and thinly disguised self-promotion for each of the local businesses.

Then she clicked on the third file. And her blood chilled to ice, clogging in her veins.

Seth had interviewed the TV producers. The article wasn't particularly hard-hitting or illuminating. And it was well edited. But one paragraph popped out.

"Everyone has a story, and Loon Lake is especially rich. We want to hear all the tales."

They'd already interviewed Seth and Ashley. What would happen when they spoke with Zach or Lonnie? At least she was confident in Grant and Molly. They really didn't have any superstitious folklore to add. Could she keep the crew away from the other locals? Maybe she could persuade the men to decline if she reminded them about their ill-fated treasure hunt that had landed them in jail for a few hours. Their records had been quickly expunged when Christopher had dropped all charges. But did the men really want to put attention back on their epic screwup?

*Everyone has a story to tell.*

Not her. Elise was carefully curating what filtered into the town's archives. Her story was only about the town, or at least of her vision of it.

"Hey? How's it looking?" Seth called.

She cleared her throat and clicked on another file. "So far, so good. No changes."

"Great. I'm almost done here, and we can start printing. It shouldn't take too long to print and assemble. Thanks for helping."

"Don't thank me. It's what we do, isn't it?" She called back. But she might as well have internalized the question. Taking care of each other was what Loon Lake was all about.

She'd do her part and remind a few select people about their best interests as well.

*Chapter Eleven*

s the sun rose over the lake the next morning, the sky slowly changed from inky blue to warm purple to soft pink, fading into a bright light blue and Seth parked in the inn's circular drive. The valet stand was closed by the time he grabbed the newspapers off the backseat. He strode into the building via the revolving door, juggling the heavy bundle in his arms and scanning his surroundings. Only one attendant worked the front desk. The suit-clad man tipped his head in greeting, and Seth returned the gesture with a smile. The lobby was quiet, almost solemn in the early hours. He hated to break the peace with any noise.

Seth tiptoed toward the newsstand to add this week's edition of *Loon Lake Life* to the collection. Set to one side of the sweeping grand staircase, the spot was semi-secluded. A guest entering the lobby from the front doors would not see him, but he was in clear sight of the restaurant. With no one coming or going in any direction, he was glad for the chance to take his time with his task and replay the night before.

While last night might not have been a movie-worthy first date, he felt good about what had happened. They had enjoyed a few laughs and worked late into the night. She had volunteered to help him deliver, but he had refused.

She had a full day of work ahead, and he could take the morning off. He'd said good night to her at one in the morning and finished sorting his deliveries and loading his car. And he hadn't stopped regretting the moment he stepped away instead of pulling her into his arms and pressing his lips to hers. Had she wanted to be kissed? He couldn't stop staring at her mouth.

While he prayed Zach's friend zone claims were an exaggeration, he hadn't been willing to risk it all by making a move last night. At his first stop, the boardwalk, he'd replayed the moments just before he brought up the pdfs. He really thought she felt the electricity between them.

After he set the stacks outside each shop on the boardwalk, making several trips from his car to the stores, he pushed aside all of the what-ifs and worries.

He floated on air. He felt nothing but joy and a sense of lightness. When he did finally sleep, he knew he'd have wonderful dreams. Because she'd said yes and hadn't backed down in front of others. Things were changing, and he happily followed her lead. As the hours passed, he understood what she hadn't said. She wasn't feeling a rush to change their status because she must want a big moment.

He'd give her a romantic gesture, something extraordinary and special. She deserved no less. He was thrilled that she didn't hide. He was proud to be seen with her, but he vowed not to push too far, too fast. He'd take all the time required to get the girl.

The top three newspapers slid off the stand and onto the tile floor. Exhaustion was catching up with him. He'd thought he'd done a decent job of stacking them, but must have misjudged. He bent down and grabbed the errant pages, neatly stacked them on top of the others. Scanning the front page of

*Loon Lake Life* as he did, he saw more than his labor but the strides he'd made towards his future. A future that included her.

The lead article was an interview with Kate and Pete. It had been a fun turning of the tables, and he agreed with their sentiment about the need and value for personal storytelling. While Elise had expressed concerns about Ashley hijacking the project with her ghost, Elise couldn't have known how he had encouraged Ashley and how her story had resonated with him. At the start of Soupy, he had only had Dad's support. If his father hadn't listened to his story, he would have had a much dimmer life, not nearly as full of dreaming and creating and possibilities.

Heavy work boots thudded against the lobby's tile floor.

Seth leaned around the staircase to survey the scene.

Mr. Willie strode at his typical quick pace, unconcerned about disturbing the stillness in the room. In a few broad steps, he disappeared.

He moved so swiftly that he could have floated. Had Seth imagined the other man's presence? Was Mr. Willie real or an apparition? Seth shuddered. Ashley's ghost stuck to the lighthouse. He wouldn't invent another one in the inn.

*Skulkers gonna skulk.*

Zach's phrase to describe the inn's caretaker popped into Seth's brain. Mr. Willie was a longtime resident and yet a mystery. He'd been in the background for as long as Seth could remember. Mr. Willie was a constant, yet he'd never been approachable. His stoic nature lent itself to wild stories from children about harsh treatment for trespassers on the property. Although thinking back, Seth wouldn't have been surprised if Ashley's late father, Xavier, had started those rumors to keep the kids from attempting vandalism or youthful pranks on his land.

Mr. Willie remained removed from the greater community, always on the periphery. Which was a shame for Seth because if anyone had seen anything suspicious, Mr. Willie would have. Seth had always been too reticent to push when it seemed that the man didn't hear him calling.

Maybe if Seth wanted different results, he needed different methods.

Seth waved at the front desk clerk and raced out the front door.

Mr. Willie headed towards the pine forest between the inn and its nearest neighbor, the tour boat company.

Seth followed. Should he call out now? Or would Mr. Willie simply ignore him? A slight breeze rustled the pine branches as Seth crunched fallen needles underfoot. If the lobby had been like a church, the forest was a mausoleum. He hated to disturb the peace with a yell.

Something cracked and crunched.

Seth froze. The hair on the back of his neck raised, and he shuddered, hating the sense of being watched. Mr. Willie hadn't slowed or turned around. He wasn't paying any attention to Seth. But the skin-crawling awareness didn't abate.

A branch snapped, the crack as loud as thunder and equally as unwelcome in the present circumstances.

Seth hung back and crouched, hiding behind the nearest tree trunk as much as possible. With its limbs thinning as it reached for the sky, he didn't have a lot of cover. He chose a tree almost as thick as he was wide. His heartbeat raced, and his blood thrummed in his veins. If he'd been tired moments before, the shock of the noise had snapped him to attention.

Mr. Willie stopped, too.

From a hundred yards ahead, he turned, his brow wrinkled. His neck twisted in one direction and the other, skimming past Seth's hiding spot. And then Mr. Willie continued ahead.

Now Seth spotted Mr. Willie's destination: the Hale

family cemetery on the hill rising just ahead. Seth could easily follow the groundskeeper and have a moment alone. He had questions only Mr. Willie could answer.

But Seth didn't move. His limbs turned to lead, and his stomach twisted.

Heavy, plodding steps, completely oblivious to the tranquility they were destroying, trudged through the forest.

"Hey, where did he go?" A deep voice asked.

"I don't know," a woman's voice answered.

"Can we call for backup?" the first voice asked.

If Seth weren't totally disoriented, he'd think he was listening to Kate and Pete. They weren't here. They'd gone back to LA for the week. Lack of sleep was playing major mind games on Seth.

"He's the key to this whole thing," the man said. "We can't lose him."

Were they talking about Seth? Was he in danger? Because of Soupy?

"Let's just follow," the woman said. "Keep to the tree line."

Seth remained hidden in place. The voices hadn't said who they were following. He wanted to be sure he wasn't the subject of surveillance. But what was Mr. Willie involved with if shadowy figures tailed him?

The footsteps grew louder, crunching past.

He spotted two hooded figures, one carrying a camera.

Seth held his breath until the pair, with faces obscured, disappeared in the direction of Mr. Willie.

The cameras were gone. Or so he'd been told. Only a scientific crew was supposed to be staying behind. The hoodie-clad stalkers didn't seem very professional to Seth. But the camera they carried didn't look cheap. If the pair chasing after Mr. Willie were amateurs, they might be using their phones to film. One held a device not too dissimilar from those used by Kate and Pete's crew. Scientists shouldn't be chasing down a person while disguising themselves. Observation and experimentation were the standards for that field.

Who was following Mr. Willie? And why? A rogue pair of Soupy hunters? He'd think his shop would be their first stop, or at least they'd reach out to Grant. In the past, curious visitors had done so, and he'd given Seth a heads-up.

But this situation was different. Seth's stomach churned, and his palms went clammy. He couldn't shake his biggest worry about the most obvious identity of the people—crewmembers working for Kate and Pete.

If the crew wasn't being honest about their current whereabouts, Seth worried. He had to deliver Soupy. He hated to think the documentary would explore some other angle or prove someone else's theory. He had to tell Elise.

* * *

Elise should have stayed at the shop. She never liked a half-finished project or a missed opportunity. Leaving before finishing the deliveries was both. Helping him was the best excuse possible to spend time together. Sure, she'd left at his insistence and headed home to nap for a few hours. But she hadn't rested.

Instead, she'd tossed and turned, torturing herself over the non-kiss. Had she misread the situation? The second she'd uttered the whole spiel about not rushing ahead, she'd wished she could take back everything she'd said. But he hadn't argued. He'd stepped back, and the spell had broken. So, after she helped him print, she loaded her car and left when he offered. She'd needed space to think and cool off.

Because, with reflection, she'd almost made a foolhardy choice for no good reason other than the heat of a moment. She liked him. He wasn't going anywhere. Neither was she.

They had time. And she'd rather avoid becoming a B-story for the documentary crew. She was not interested in being a sideshow.

Nor could she confuse her feelings for him with the role he'd requested. For the time being at least, she was in control and had to take the lead. A real relationship demanded vulnerability and openness, which she didn't think she had. So she got out of bed, showered, and went to work as the sun rose over the lake.

She slipped her key into the front door of the log cabin, readjusting the bundle of newspapers under her arm. She still had a couple of hours before the first tour of the day. She liked getting into the museum early to go through reservations and emails, check the mail, pay bills, and all the other little tasks that added up to a busy day if not handled effectively and efficiently.

In the past couple weeks, with the added pressure of the TV crew, she had let everything pile up behind the welcome desk. She was glad to get the chance to tackle all of her to-dos in one dedicated morning.

If she could stop floating back to last night's date...

Seth had been appreciative of her help. She'd worried that falling into their usual role of helpmates would crush whatever was growing between them. She didn't want to just be his taskmaster or his temporary manager. With both in mind, she had avoided asking any questions about the interview with Kate and Pete. Her suspicions were hers alone, and she didn't need to burden anyone else.

She hadn't found any issues in the rest of his articles. She'd forgotten how well he'd done in school. He was easy to discount and overlook. He didn't proclaim his successes or boast about his wins. He kept to the background during a lot of their adolescence. But he was book smart and clever with words. His kindness was so impressive, and his capacity for caring was endless. Always supporting others, including those like Zach who might not deserve him, presented the illusion that he was a passive follower. But he could be formidable if he ever decided. She'd like to be there when he did.

She left the door ajar as she entered, stepping in sideways and setting the bundle of newspapers on the welcome desk. Her foot kicked something.

Frowning, she carefully shut the door before retrieving the plain white envelope. It was unsealed. She opened it and pulled out a slip of lined paper, too small for a standard notebook but the size of a notepad with a rough tear along the top. She unfolded the page.

*TURN OFF THE CAMERAS* was scrawled in capital letters and sloppy writing. The hurried print struck her as angry and threatening. Her heartbeat pounded.

She checked the door to be sure she'd closed it securely and tiptoed to one of the few windows in the building. She glanced outside but spotted nothing unusual in the front yard. Had someone been watching her? Waiting for her? She shuddered.

The note hadn't been an obvious threat, but she couldn't shake the dread that settled over her. She read the slip again. Yes, she had inserted the words OR ELSE, but why leave a note if you didn't expect a confrontation? She wished she had salt to throw over her shoulder. Maybe some sage to burn in the log cabin. She was the least superstitious person in town, but maybe that was only because she had been living in ignorance.

She dragged in a deep breath and made her way back to the front desk. She was playing out worst-case scenarios based on nothing. Paranoia wasn't her style. There were no security cameras on the property because there had never been a need. She rolled her neck from one side to the other. If she had some sort of surveillance, she might have had a chance at catching a glimpse of the person. Should she reach out to Tim?

He'd asked her to keep him in the loop. She didn't know what he'd be able to do. By telling him about the threat, she worried she highlighted her incompetence. At the moment, she was following the demands. The cameras were off, and the crew had left, at least for a short while. So the mystery note writer would be satisfied.

She didn't need to involve anyone else and didn't need to tell the police. Which was good. She didn't want to look foolish or hysterical.

But something still felt off. She grabbed her cell phone and her keys out of her purse. The note had reminded her of the skin-crawling feeling of worry that she hadn't been able to fully expunge since Ashley's interview. The cameras were gone, but the science crew was still here. Right?

She slipped through the back door and locked it behind herself. She hadn't seen anyone taking samples or images from her spot on the lake. Shouldn't she see someone? She was tempted to call Christopher and ask him if the crew was still at the cottage, his quaint nickname for his home in the half-converted stables. Would she worry him?

Because her biggest fear was that they were all still being watched and filmed. The museum didn't have a camera focused on the lake. She walked the perimeter, confirming no other devices had been added after the fact and without her knowledge.

They'd signed consent forms, so they couldn't revoke access. But what was the true scope of the project?

Seth's Soupy might have brought them here, but would the Timber Triangle, Ashley's ghost, or the treasure spark a new idea? A reality show would not make the town look good, but of all of them, Seth would look the worst. She couldn't let that happen.

It was easy to assume nothing bad would happen. And for almost ten months, the town had been quiet. But last summer's fires, abductions, and explosions removed any doubt that trouble didn't strike in their small town. She'd rather stay ahead of the potential for danger and misdeeds.

Grabbing her phone, she pulled up the group text. **We need to meet at the inn.** She hit send. In seconds, she'd had thumbs-up and hearts.

**Ashley Hale-Lewis: YES.**

The immediate response chilled Elise to her bones. With the sun barely breaking the horizon, she expected to wait at least an hour for a response. Ashley was awake and checking her phone. Had she received a note?

**Ashley Hale-Lewis: When?**

**On my way**. Elise texted back.

With her keys and her phone, she made her way back to her car and hopped in the driver's seat. She'd waste no time. Either they'd all come up with a plan, or she'd know her emotions got the better of her after a poor night's sleep. Then she'd get back to work.

Chapter Twelve

In the office on the top floor of the inn, Seth felt refreshed in spite of himself. He'd headed home for a shower and had just finished when he got the text asking to meet at the inn. He was glad for it. He didn't have to figure out who to tell or how to explain what he had seen in the woods. He could meet with everyone at once and share the odd scene he'd witnessed. He'd leave the situation in capable, analytical hands. And then he'd go home for an overdue nap.

Maybe he'd read too much into the whole situation. Exhaustion could warp the mind and perception. Or he had witnessed something strange. He couldn't keep the encounter to himself. At least, with his friends, he trusted honesty wouldn't be met with ridicule.

"Thanks for meeting on such short notice," Elise said to the group.

Ashley and Christopher sat behind the desk, Mr. Willie standing nearby. Molly had taken a position in one of the leather club chairs and offered the other to Elise when she entered. But she had declined.

Now she paced the room. Seth stood near the front windows, trying to offer support without crowding her.

A knock sounded on the corner door.

"Sorry," Christopher said and stood. "I ordered a coffee service." He crossed to the door and opened it, letting a staff member carry the tray to the desk before departing. The college-age kid huffed and puffed as he departed. The tight spiral staircase descended directly to the first floor, a quick passage for the boss to get anywhere fast.

"Please, help yourselves, and then we can get to business," Christopher said. "I'm guessing we're all here to talk about the damaged cameras."

Elise drew back her chin.

Seth studied the others, all nodding in unison as they poured themselves full mugs.

"No," Elise said, the word short and tense.

He noticed her tight shoulders, the tension in her neck. He didn't know about any vandalism. But he wasn't always in the loop like Elise.

"Why did you call the meeting?" Ashley asked, taking her seat.

"I... I..." Elise stammered.

Seth gaped. She was never unaware or unsure. He could step up for her and give her a second to compose herself. "What happened with the cameras?"

"Mr. Willie found the damage this morning on his rounds. The lighthouse camera was disconnected," Ashley said.

"More than that." Mr. Willie snorted. "The cords were sliced with a knife, a clean break. Sabotage."

Sabotage. The word dumbfounded Seth. Sure, he knew the definition. He'd only heard it spoken on TV or in movies. No one had ever used the word in real life.

"That's only a little better than what happened to me and Grant," Molly said. "He's on his way. We heard a sound early this morning at the sawmill and saw a hooded figure run away. The camera on the pier was smashed. He's checking the boathouse now." She shuddered. "I'm worried about what he'll find. When I went outside, the camera was on the ground in pieces," Molly continued. "It looked...personal. Overkill."

Seth's heart sank. The cameras were supposed to be for constant surveillance. While he'd never had any encounters above the water, he'd been glad for the attempt at capturing as much footage as possible. Any discrepancies could be cross-referenced. Not anymore. Someone wanted to ruin his big moment? Why?

"Who would do this?" Elise asked. "It makes no sense."

"I have been waiting all morning for the research crew still staying at the cottage to come and speak with me," Christopher said. "They are monitoring those feeds. Haven't they noticed the screens are black or static?"

"How much do you suppose we'll be liable for?" Molly asked.

Mr. Willie made the sign of the cross.

Ashley gulped. "I can't imagine any of us has a few hundred thousand dollars lying around to cover the costs."

"Let's not jump to conclusions," Elise said. "We have no idea how much the equipment costs. For all we know, the production is well insured, and the damages will be handled without us. The best first step is to file police reports. I got a note this morning at the museum. I don't have any surveillance or any cameras for the project, so I don't know who slipped it under the door. It just said *Turn off the cameras.*"

"Or...what?" Christopher asked.

Elise shrugged.

The room fell silent.

Seth wanted Soupy to help the town, not hurt it. Why would someone want the cameras off? Why would they go to extremes to do so themselves? Maybe the crew he saw this morning was already aware of the situation and was doing their own investigation.

He didn't want to keep secrets from the group, but he also didn't want to stoke up any paranoia. He didn't know what he saw. He'd keep his mouth shut. The real problems—and threat—were far more important.

The door slammed against the wall.

Seth jumped and turned toward the main entrance.

"I'm sorry," Zach said, panting. "I didn't want to do it. I was blackmailed." He rushed inside—a blur of fluorescent colors—and shut the door, doubling over and holding his sides.

"Do what?" Seth asked.

Zach scrunched up his face.

"I knew you were up to something at the parade," Elise said, shaking her head. "You wouldn't meet my gaze and kept running off. I forgave you for Seth's sake. I should have pushed harder for the truth."

Zach turned red. "I know. I'm sorry." He straightened. "Really. I feel terrible."

"You should. We're potentially liable for a massive amount of money," Christopher said.

"What were you being blackmailed about?" Molly asked.

"It's a...ugh...topic of a... sensitive nature," Zach said, dragging out the words and shifting his weight from foot to foot.

"Really?" Ashley leaned forward at the desk, her eyes widening.

Christopher held up a hand. "No, we don't want to hear about whatever exploits this loathsome lothario has been involved in." He shuddered. "Taking him seriously while he's dressed like that is hard enough."

Seth frowned. He liked Zach's nostalgic uniform. The

fluorescent shirt was set off by the overalls. It was fun and off-beat. Like him. But what he was saying didn't align with the friend Seth had always counted on. Blackmailed into a crime?

"What happened?" Molly asked.

"Probably some of our guests have been subjected to texts of an explicit manner that have been intercepted," Christopher said, answering for Zach as he scrunched his face like he could make himself disappear.

"Oh." Ashley recoiled and curled her upper lip.

"It's not like *that*," Zach stressed, stuffing his fists into his overall pockets.

"And you were susceptible because things are now getting serious with the woman from the dairy? A business associate turned more, and she'd be upset to find out?" Molly asked.

"It all happened before we got serious. We weren't togeth-er," Zach said. "But, yeah. That's the extent of it."

"Who could be blackmailing you?" Elise asked.

Zach lifted a shoulder. "It could be quite a few people."

Christopher groaned. "How many people have received undesired pictures of your....down there? Are you using the inn as some sort of hunting ground?"

"Slow down, Sheriff Lewis. It's not like that!" Zach shuddered. "You want the truth? Fine. Here goes." He blew out a heavy breath. "I was on a break with Mary and was lonely. I met a woman at the bar at the inn. She was cute. I thought we hit it off because we exchanged phone numbers. We start texting. It was heating up. I sent her a selfie."

"Your face in the photo doesn't make it less gross," Ashley said with a sad shake of her head.

"Look, I was shirtless, but I was wearing these." Zach tugged at the strap on his white overalls.

"Like a sad, Dexy's Midnight Runners cover band," Christopher murmured, loud enough for the room to snicker.

Zach flared his nostrils. "Please, make the jokes because

that's really helpful and illuminating. Forget all the times I've helped the people in this room, and torture me a little. It's fine."

Seth agreed and was glad the others quieted down. Elise had every reason to be angry with Zach, but the others piling on wasn't warranted. Seth studied the room, hoping for a clue about where the story was going. Because he couldn't make sense of any of the tale. If Zach and the woman hit it off, what was the problem? An unexpected photo in return? "I don't get it. What happened? You send her a picture and then?"

"And I asked for her to send a picture in return. That's when it got embarrassing." Zach's cheeks reddened.

"She showed it to everyone? The picture you got wasn't her? You couldn't have been catfished if you met her in person?" Seth asked.

"Except, I was." Zach hung his head. "Turns out, she was the chaperone for her grandmother and her friends on a ladies' trip. The older women were texting me the whole time. They sent back a group photo. They'd grabbed the granddaughter's phone when she went upstairs to grab someone's reading glasses and then kept asking her to run errands so she wouldn't realize it was gone."

"Why would one of them blackmail you now?" Elise asked. "Or was it the woman? Was she mad you didn't pursue her? I'm so confused here."

Zach held up both hands in surrender. "Their group selfie was sent from the fire pit outside the inn. They were quite public. Anyone could have heard about what was going on and used it against me."

"I don't understand why you were blackmailed over something so silly?" Molly asked.

Seth was glad Molly was there. Without years of history, she might be the only person capable of asking the right questions without bias.

Zach shuddered. "It's not me I'm worried about. Or it wasn't... I am so sorry, Elise. Please don't go to the police," he managed between shallow breaths.

"Zach, you have caused thousands of dollars of damage. I can't cover that up," Elise said.

"Not that much, surely," Zach said. "How much can a flatbed trailer cost? Not thousands. And it looked functional once it was hauled out of the lake."

Seth twisted his neck, taking in the confused looks. Good, he wasn't the only person shocked by Zach's sudden appearance and contradictory confession. "What are you talking about?" he asked his friend.

"I got a threatening note, advising me to ruin the parade, or some information I would prefer not become public would be shared all over town. I tampered with the float," Zach said.

"You did that on purpose?" Seth asked.

Zach nodded.

No wonder Zach had advised Seth against standing on the float.

"You were advised to do what exactly?" Molly asked.

"Derail the parade and mess with the filming along the route. Play copyrighted music over the sound system so the footage couldn't be used. I'm sorry, Seth," Zach said.

"Oh," Seth said. He wasn't sure how to feel. Glad his friend hadn't been involved in the camera destruction but sad to realize Seth had been the target. One portion of the sabotage was personal.

"Zach, we have bigger issues at hand than the parade," Elise said. "But you owe me the apology for that. The bigger problem is that the cameras set up around town have been damaged. We're going to be liable for thousands of dollars of damage. Do you know anything about that?"

Zach paled and gulped. "What? The cameras are broken? Oh, and you thought I confessed to that?"

"I don't like that you were blackmailed into acting against a friend. It was a minor sort of infraction, but why didn't you come to any of us?" Christopher asked, crossing his arms over his chest. "This seems so trivial."

Zach stuffed his hands into his overall pockets. "I wasn't thinking. I was feeling."

Seth could understand that.

"Explain why. We need answers. You're a liability," Christopher said. "If any tiny, unimportant thing can get you to commit property damage, you can't be trusted."

"Because..." Zach darted his gaze side to side, searching. "I'm going to be a dad."

"Congratulations." Seth strode across the room and embraced his friend. Wonderful news should be cherished and celebrated.

Zach didn't return the hug. He stood like a statue.

"What's wrong?" Seth asked, pulling away.

"If Mary finds out about the woman at the bar, she might reconsider our attempt at being together. Officially," Zach said.

"Doesn't she have a right to know?" Christopher asked. "You were sending crude images to other women indiscriminately."

Ashley shook her head at her husband. "Get mad at him for using our inn as a meat market, sure, but let's ease up on the hyperbole."

From the corner of his gaze, Seth spotted Christopher's eyeroll. Seth kept his arm around Zach's shoulders. He'd support his friend in any way he could. "It's all behind us now. But if you didn't destroy the cameras, who did? Who had motive?"

"I hate to say it, but I know we're all thinking it," Ashley said.

Elise groaned. "The Prims are behind bars. What could

they hope to gain from ruining the project? Who could they be working with in town?"

"Notoriety. Maybe some money," Ashley said with a shrug. "Who knows why the Prims do what they do?"

"Why not Leonard Baird?" Molly asked with a shudder.

While Ashley's life had been endangered by Steve and Carl Prim, Molly was threatened by their lawyer, Leonard Baird.

"Didn't you hear?" Elise asked. "He passed six months ago in jail. Heart attack."

"Oh," Molly murmured, her brow furrowed.

Seth understood confused feelings. He'd dealt with his share concerning that trio.

"It's probably worth a meeting with Steve and Carl," Ashley said. "To be sure it's not them. And maybe to ascertain what they know about the TV show."

Elise nodded. "Good point. I'll go. You call the police and report what happened. I don't know if any of us will be liable to cover the costs of the damage, but we can figure that out later."

"Before we disband," Christopher said. "Elise? Are you okay? What are you thinking?"

Elise blushed. "I'm worried we're being used by Kate and Pete. I haven't seen any of their crew around town. Aren't they supposed to be conducting experiments? Are they just holed up inside the cottage watching the cameras?" She shuddered. "Something feels off."

"Like a reality show?" Ashley asked. "My dad would roll in his grave if we'd buried him. I suppose, since we spread his ashes, he might toss up the currents in the lake."

"If that's what they are after, the Prims would definitely have been approached," Christopher said. "You should see them."

"What do you want us to do?" Seth asked.

Elise met his gaze with a dazed look he'd never seen before. She looked lost and a little scared.

"Come on, John Candy, give us our orders," he teased. "Coach us."

Murmurs echoed in the room at the inside joke.

She rolled her eyes. "I guess we need to head to the sheriff's office to file a report and find out about visiting the Prims. We need answers."

Seth hoped they'd find some. He had a sinking feeling that questioning Steve and Carl would only add to the frustration and chaos.

"Seth, can you come with me?" Elise asked.

He'd go with her anywhere. "Always."

"Keep us posted?" Christopher asked.

"We will," Seth vowed.

The door opened.

Grant appeared. "Are you going after the podcast guy?"

Doubled over and panting, he must have run the mile from the boathouse.

"Podcast guy? What are you talking about?" Elise asked.

She used her deliberate question voice. The one she employed when she had no idea what someone was talking about and wanted them to spill all the details. She'd be listening carefully to each syllable.

"Last year, when I first took over, I was at the courthouse on the day of the first hearing. Some guy was talking into a microphone. Said something about a podcast called *Sins of the Father*. I ducked out as soon as I could. Didn't want him to recognize me and try to interview me," Grant said, between gulping breaths.

"Has anyone heard about this before?" Elise asked the room.

"Sorry, I should have mentioned it," Grant replied. "I know the Prims are a touchy subject. I've been listening for business purposes. In case any detail I should know slipped in."

Grant was accepted so swiftly into the community that it was easy to forget he remained a relative newcomer. He might err on the side of caution, not wanting to rile anyone up. "Really, I meant no harm. Accidental lie of omission." Grant crossed his heart. "I've been following everything about the Prims, so I'm not caught off guard again."

The conversation took a dangerous turn. Christopher had missed clues, and Molly nearly paid the price with her life.

Seth saw his confusion and shock mirrored on the faces around him. Then a memory flashed. The muffled voices coming from Grant's phone at the dock. His hesitance at the gala, like he'd held himself back from saying something. "Sounds like something else to investigate. We'd better not waste any time."

Elise met his gaze.

For a moment, she looked lost and bewildered. Vulnerable. He hated seeing her as anything other than totally competent and in charge. He stepped forward and interlaced their fingers. He'd take charge for her. She could count on him just as much as he depended on her. They were a team.

"We'll take care of this and be in touch. If anyone sees or hears anything, let's all keep in contact on the group text," he said. And with a nod, he left the room with Elise.

* * *

Elise wished she were as unaffected as her public persona. Maybe others would balk and scoff at the description, considering it the same as being branded a witch by the Puritans, but not her. Unfeeling meant undisturbed. Peaceful.

Reality sucked. Anxious, hot, and very bothered. She suffered emotions all too well. Did she still present as the ice queen to the world at large? That would be a small consolation.

Seth had seen through her unaffected bravado. In the inn's office, surrounded by a crowd of friends, he'd looked at her with concern, and she'd nearly buckled. If he hadn't teased her, snapping her out of her worried daze, would he have rushed across the crowded room to catch her?

Being truly seen by him was oddly intimate. She didn't mind sharing her vulnerability because she trusted him. Others might use her fears as a weakness. Not Seth. And, in kind, he depended on her.

Squaring her shoulders, she paused outside the sheriff's office. "Ready?"

He nodded and opened the door.

She entered first.

As far as centers for justice went, the front of the station was cozy. A mismatched collection of reupholstered chairs created a waiting area in the front. A ceramic lamp sat on the composite front counter, casting a soft glow. The cracked, bulbous table lamp was repurposed, just like the chairs. And yet, the wear in the item gave a sense of history and home. Not exactly appropriate for a sheriff's station, but almost inevitable for the waste not, want not community.

Behind the counter, the large room had several tables pushed together, a scattering of computers and files on each. A large desk in the corner commanded attention due to its size and position. It was allocated for Sheriff Hanks. The piece was substantial, a better fit for the library of an English country home.

A doorway in the back corner led to the two-cell jail. No doubt it would be concrete block construction with metal bars. Before last summer, the jail hadn't held anyone for a crime worse than disorderly conduct; those offenders—usually Lonnie—were typically released within a few hours.

"Good morning," Elise called as she strode to the counter.

From his desk in the corner, Sheriff Hanks got to his feet. "Hello," he replied, hurrying to the front. "To what do I owe the pleasure of this visit?"

Elise shot Seth a look. She had two orders of business. Did she dare add a third? Zach's betrayal burned. He needed to grow up and stop making everyone's life complicated because of his emotional immaturity. She doubted a baby would change him. But he didn't deserve a record for his treachery.

"We need to file a report for the damage to the TV cameras," Seth said.

Sheriff Hanks lifted his bushy eyebrows. "Oh?"

Elise nodded, finding her voice again. "And we need to visit the Prims."

"Oh." Sheriff Hanks deflated. "The first is easy enough." At the counter, he reached for a clipboard and a form. "I'll need to take down the applicable information and visit the scene."

"Scenes," Elise corrected. "The sawmill, the lighthouse, and the boathouse."

"Why are you telling me? Are the property owners aware of the situation?" Sheriff Hanks asked.

"Yes, and waiting for you," Elise said. "We want to gather all the proper evidence for insurance."

"Fair enough." Sheriff Hanks jotted down a few notes. "I'll call them before I head over." He raised his gaze. "Why do you want to see the Prims?"

"To make sure they aren't involved," Seth said.

"Let me put your minds at ease," Sheriff Hanks raised a hand, "they aren't. They can't be. This isn't TV. The Prims don't operate a criminal enterprise. They have no associates. No one is carrying out their orders on the outside."

"Well that's what we thought before the situation with

Mr. Baird and the sawmill, right?" Elise offered. She hoped her half-hearted smile softened the blow..

Sheriff Hanks shifted his weight and frowned.

"And, apparently, a podcast is detailing the Prims' case," Seth said.

Sheriff Hanks scrubbed his hands over his face. "Really? Why can't civilians leave the police work to trained law enforcement professionals?"

Elise shrugged. "We aren't here to get in your way. We'd like to talk to Steve and Carl. Face to face. Get an understanding of what they are involved with and how much. If the sabotage is tied into their case because of an unhinged fanatic, we all need to know. Don't we?"

"I suppose," Sheriff Hanks muttered. "Hold on a second, I'll give the corrections facility a call."

"Thank you," Elise replied.

With a shake of his head, Sheriff Hanks retreated across the room.

She got it. Bad decision to visit the Prims. If she had another choice, she'd make it. But she wasn't the type to mope around when she could take action.

"Shall we sit?" Seth asked.

Elise studied the chairs by the window, in full view of the street. If she sat, she'd be easy to spot to anyone passing by. Of course, the biggest gossip in town, Zach, already knew she was here.

The door opened, saving her a response.

Tim appeared in the doorway, holding a bag and a tray with two coffees. "Who wants bagels with Burt?" he asked as he entered and stopped short. "Oh. Elise. Seth. Hi. What are you doing here?" The broad grin slipped off his face.

Seth opened his mouth.

"Never mind." Tim cut him off. "Don't tell me. Not my

business. I stop in once a week to see if there is anything my office can assist with. And I bring breakfast."

Elise's eye twitched from the stress of not rolling. Tim was best friends with Sheriff Hanks. Until the mayoral election, no one would have thought twice about Tim stopping by. In a small community, the appearance of impropriety was hard to avoid as friendships had deep roots. She appreciated the complicated navigation of the ties between duty and loyalty in the new role.

"I am glad I bumped into you, Elise," Tim said.

"Oh?" she asked.

"Yes, I've been hearing a lot of buzz from your events. I know you don't have anything else planned this year." Tim emphasized the last two words.

Elise held her breath. She didn't want Tim to reveal her premiere party idea to Seth.

"Could you add another town-wide activity to the calendar soon?" Tim asked. "Maybe think about it. The gala, fun run, and parade really got a lot of attention."

"Oh." Her ears burned. Being the punchline of a joke wasn't her goal. Visit Loon Lake and gawk at the wacky locals was hardly a tourism slogan.

"In fact," Tim continued, "I've received several inquiries about the foundation and how to donate online."

*Could that be true?*

"I've heard the same from the guests on my tours," Seth added. "If you look in the inn's guest book, you'll see a lot of *best summer ever* comments."

Her heart skipped a beat. Without her governance, her events had gone sideways. Or maybe that was just her opinion. Visitors said otherwise. Perhaps she could ease up on her need for perfection. And then she could have a life.

"Okay, Carl is a no," Sheriff Hanks announced.

His words sliced through her thoughts. She raised her gaze to the man crossing the room.

"Steve already added you both to his approved visitors list. You'll need to wait two business days for the request to process," Sheriff Hanks said.

Had Steve anticipated a visit? *Did that incriminate him in the sabotage?* She hated the unknown and wanted to be ready for whatever happened.

But no conjecture promised the answers she'd need. She'd only learn that from a face-to-face visit. Steve might have been hiding nefarious deeds on behalf of his father. But he'd never backed down from a question asked point-blank.

Tim gasped. "You're visiting Steve? Really?"

Elise shrugged.

Sheriff Hanks shook his head.

"It's only that we—" Seth said.

"Nope, no. Sorry." Tim held up his hands. "Not my business, and I don't want to know. Just be careful?"

Elise nodded. A shiver slipped down her spine, but she fought to stand still. Visiting a kidnapper in prison wasn't ideal. Facing someone she'd known forever who remained a stranger was even harder. But she wouldn't lose her nerve with everything on the line.

# Chapter Thirteen

T he next couple of days passed quickly and, luckily, without any other incident. Seth almost forgot about Zach's betrayal. The TV crew hadn't contacted him or anyone else regarding the damage to the cameras and equipment. Did they not notice? Shouldn't the research crew be aware?

Every day, Seth practiced what he'd say if Kate and Pete called him or, worse, strolled into the store. But he couldn't find the words. This scenario—not that he ever could have imagined it—was exactly why he'd asked Elise to be his John Candy.

The police reports had been filed. Elise had taken care of everything on their end. He was grateful but also frustrated. The more she worked to clean up his mess, the more he worried that he'd been shoved back into the friend zone.

If there was such a thing as a window of opportunity for making a move, he worried the opening was less than an inch. He hadn't figured out a romantic gesture grand enough to earn a kiss. And at the present moment, as they drove to the jail to confront Steve Prim, he couldn't help but worry even more that he'd totally miss his shot.

The day was not set up for a moment of passion. From the corner of his eye, he studied her. Since he'd picked her up twenty minutes ago, he hadn't been able to get more than a yes or no answer from her in response to any of his questions. Was she as apprehensive as he was about coming face-to-face with Steve?

After the events of last summer and Zach's confession, Seth felt off balance. How well did any of them really know each other? They'd grown up together, but maybe that was part of the problem. Their history trapped them in their high school roles, rather than allowing them to see one another for who they had become.

Zach had been a saboteur hiding in plain sight. Seth understood the how and why of the manipulation as soon as Zach came clean. Steve, however, remained a mystery.

"Found it," Elise announced.

Seth glanced over at her in the shotgun seat.

She waved her phone and fiddled with the sound system.

His mind was blank. What had she been looking for? Answers? He needed some desperately.

"The podcast?" she supplied. "Sorry to be so quiet. And to take so long. I didn't anticipate how many podcasts would use the word sin in their title."

He chuckled. Using a vice as a keyword wouldn't be his choice. But neither would starting up an internet radio show. Zach had floated the idea about creating one for Soupy. Seth hadn't seen the point. He'd rather do the documentary and maintain his website and tours, collecting tips the old-fashioned way.

"Ready?" Elise asked.

Seth snapped back to the present. He was driving a car. He had to focus. "Sure."

Elise tapped a button on her phone, and organ music played over the car stereo. She snorted. "Rather grand."

He smiled in agreement.

"Welcome to *Sins of the Father*," a deep voice intoned. "I'm Chad Whirl, and for the past year, I have been following a curious case in a quaint community."

"Can't fault his alliteration." Seth tightened his grip on the steering wheel, bracing for the man's interpretation of their town. He'd learned that outsiders didn't always appreciate the close-knit nature of their community. Sure, Zach and Christopher might barely conceal their disdain for one another. But either man would lend a hand to help the other. That was Loon Lake. Seth had been on the receiving end of assistance more often than not.

"In a little town in the North Woods," the voice continued, leaning into a husky tone that sounded unnatural, "a father and son hid dark secrets from nosy neighbors."

"Rude," Elise muttered.

"Until the culmination of their dastardly plan nearly took the life of an unsuspecting ingenue."

"Really?" Elise's response was part gasp and part squeak. "Did Ashley give this guy a script? I can't imagine anyone else describing her like that. We're all on a collision course with middle age."

Seth swallowed his chuckle. He appreciated Elise's wry commentary.

"But was Steve truly a co-conspirator?" Chad continued. "Or merely the latest victim in a legacy of familial crime."

Organ music rose, suddenly joined by a chorus of youthful voices.

Elise hit pause. "I'm sorry. I don't think I can handle this right now. I didn't anticipate how it would feel to hear someone else's opinion of our town." She snorted. "I guess I'd better get used to it, though. The crew will make their own depiction."

"True," he said slowly. "The Prims left their own sort of legacy. It's a bad one. They've stained their name, but they'll be remembered."

"I don't think being notorious in the present will equal a mention in our town's history," she retorted.

"No, maybe not." But they would be spoken of at least for one more generation. He would never seek immortality by disgracing his family. Seth had to find Soupy to keep his father's name alive forever. And if Seth wasn't important, then he worried he had no place in her life. She was a steward for their community and couldn't waste her time.

*She didn't have to include me today*. While their present circumstances weren't romantic and wouldn't encourage him to make his move, he valued that she could have gone on her errand alone but included him. He'd focus on the matter at hand and push his feelings aside for the time being. "I'm confused by the angle of the podcast. What is the host trying to get at? Steve is a victim?"

Elise shrugged.

From the corner of his gaze, Seth studied her. She'd been close to Steve in high school. Had they dated? He'd never asked. It hadn't been his business then. Was it his business now?

"I think it will feel sort of icky to listen to him talk about our friends and neighbors," Elise said. "These are real people. I don't like the sensationalism. We know everyone involved, and thankfully, no one was hurt. Not for lack of trying on their part. Ashley's life was threatened. Molly was in danger, too."

He nodded. "I guess we'll have to talk to Steve to find out if he's involved with this. Then we'll know if the podcaster is our culprit. I don't know why he would be. I don't think we need to bring this up to Kate and Pete if he isn't involved."

"Good plan."

"Do you think the podcast is following an appeal on Steve's behalf? I can't understand why they'd start now."

Both Steve and Carl had been found guilty and sentenced. Despite a few delays, justice moved swiftly. It was strange to think about how devious a pair of neighbors had been, and that they had gone undetected for so long.

Seth reached for his travel mug and sipped his cola, clearing out the bad taste in his mouth. "I wanted to apologize again."

"For what?"

"The parade and the cameras. When I asked you to manage me, I didn't realize how complicated everything would get. Or that we'd potentially be on the hook for thousands of dollars of damage."

"We aren't. Vandalism isn't our fault. We've done everything we can to mitigate the fallout. But I'm not a fancy, hotshot attorney. I'm worried about some loophole that'll work against us in the contracts. I haven't heard anything from the crew, and we took all appropriate steps. If we have to pay, I have something in mind."

He didn't like the defeatist tone in her voice. "Then I'm sorry for that too. But mostly, I feel bad that I've taken all your time this summer when I know you have plenty to do. I have heard good feedback about your events."

"No, you heard laughter."

"Does that matter?"

She angled herself toward him. "Being laughed at or laughed with is a huge distinction. Yes, it matters a very great deal."

He wasn't sure he agreed. Being noticed was hard. Not everyone stood out. Her efforts had gotten plenty of attention. Tim had told her as much the other day. Maybe she needed to hear it a few times before she accepted what they were telling her.

"I can't be your John Candy," she murmured. "I'm letting everyone down. You most of all."

"You can't mean that. I'd be in over my head without you. You have managed me while running your own events. I owe you an apology for taking up so much of your time and attention. But I wouldn't have gotten here without you. I need you."

"I'm sure someone else would have stepped up."

"Who? Zach? Christopher?" Seth shook his head.

She didn't answer.

He took her silence for agreement. "Let's conduct our own side investigation. Starting with Steve."

* * *

Elise had only seen prisons and jails on TV. She had never imagined she'd see one firsthand. She hadn't prepared herself very well.

At least she had Seth for support.

He stepped up for her in a big way. When everything seemed to shift and slide, she didn't know where to turn. He took her hand, and she held on tight.

As Seth drove and Elise rode shotgun, she had plenty of time to think. She prepared herself to sit on the other side of glass, holding a phone to her ear. What happened was much different.

The lawyer had arranged a private room and was present. Considering Steve was sentenced to life in prison, found guilty of abduction, attempted murder, and arson, the lawyer was necessary.

She was glad not to be alone with Steve. His despicable actions last summer had been so out of character, she'd started to question whether she really knew him at all. She'd always sort of liked him. He was handsome by anyone's definition. He wasn't the smartest of their group, but where Seth's kindness fueled his natural optimism and tendency to give everyone the benefit of the doubt, Steve's gullibility made him easily swayed and a foot soldier in a nasty war. If his father hadn't radicalized him, Steve would have—eventually—turned into some other bad guy's goon.

Was he still doing his father's bidding?

As an officer ushered Elise and Seth down a hall, she shivered.

"Are you okay? Do you want my sweatshirt?" Seth asked, starting to slip an arm free of the hoodie.

She did want his sweatshirt but only to comfort herself. "I'm fine."

The officer opened the door and waved the pair into a room. Another officer stood in the corner.

At a round table in the center of the room, a petite woman sat next to Steve. His skin looked almost green under the fluorescent lights and against the orange jumpsuit. His hands were cuffed, and his feet were shackled.

Elise held her breath. She hadn't prepared to see him like this. He had never been a threat. Until he tried to kill someone. He'd been hiding in plain sight the whole time.

Was that their current problem? What didn't they see about their circumstances?

Seth pressed a hand to her lower back. "Let's sit."

She nodded, his touch grounding her in the present moment and not slipping back into recriminations of the past. She sat on a cold metal chair, stiffening on impact, and crossed her arms over her chest. "Thanks for meeting with us."

"My pleasure," Steve said with his easy-going grin. He turned to his attorney. "Can I say that?"

The lawyer frowned. "My client will not be answering any

questions about the case against him as he awaits news about his pending appeal."

Elise nodded. She figured as much. Gathering a jury of peers from the area who weren't prejudiced proved a difficult task. Finding a new set for another trial, if granted, would be almost impossible. "We are not interested in the past. We are only concerned about the present. Steve, are you working with anyone on the outside?"

"Huh? What do you mean? Like for the business? We sold that," Steve said.

The lawyer shook her head. "No. The bank handled all assets. My client has no contact or involvement with any business dealings in Loon Lake."

"Someone has destroyed the TV equipment," Seth said.

Elise sucked in a breath. She wasn't going to be so blunt and upfront with the information.

The lawyer leaned forward. "Hold on, TV? My client refuses all interviews and won't be villainized in the court of public opinion. We denied the requests from the podcaster for *Sins of the Father*, too."

"We did?" Steve asked at the same moment Seth said, "You did?"

Elise was surprised. While the case was a pretty open-and-shut scenario of greed gone wrong, the Steve she had known for years would have jumped at the chance for the attention. He'd been number two to someone else his entire life. First, in school, he'd been in the shadow of Christopher. And then, professionally, he'd been under his father's thumb.

His part in his father's dastardly plan was further proof of his inability to think for himself. He didn't want to steal a little limelight and cast aspersions on his co-defendant? Not even to help his case?

"When did the podcast first get in touch? Why didn't you speak with him?" Elise asked.

"It was months ago. I guess after Seth was on TV or something? I don't know. My lawyer said not to give any interviews," Steve said.

"Correct," the lawyer added. "Let's circle back to the original question. What camera?"

"A documentary crew has begun filming with one focus." Elise dragged out the word, eagerly studying every reaction. "Finding Soupy."

The lawyer furrowed her brow.

Steve widened his eyes, clear shock in his unschooled expression. "Does my dad know? He's always wanted to be on TV."

"He won't talk to anyone. We tried to visit him. I doubt he's aware if you weren't," Elise said.

"What is the production company? I will draft a cease and desist as soon as I leave," the lawyer said.

Elise held up a hand. "Please, stop. The TV crew is filming a project focused on Seth. No one has mentioned a word about the Prims and, as far as I'm concerned, it'll stay that way."

"Thanks, Elise," Steve said softly.

He smiled, the corners of his eyes crinkling in that soft way of his. She'd forgotten his smile. She'd always counted him as one of the good guys, someone to trust or turn to in a bad spot. In truth, he'd been a sheep. He wasn't a wolf in sheep's clothing. Just a sheep, blindly following whoever led him. Even over a cliff to his doom.

"Congrats, Seth. Is this going to finally get out the truth about Soupy?" Steve asked.

Seth grinned. "It is."

"I saw you on the news a while back. Good for you, man. Did I ever tell you about the time I saw Soupy?" Steve asked.

Elise gaped. What? He'd seen Soupy? He'd never said a word.

"No, you haven't. When was this? What happened?" Seth asked, his voice incredulous.

"About fifteen years ago, early summer. I was driving one of the tour boats out near the channel, and I saw it, a great smooth head and jaws coming out of the water," Steve said.

"And you didn't tell anyone? You weren't scared?" Seth asked.

"I was terrified, and it happened so fast, I wasn't sure what I saw. It came up," Steve lifted his linked hands, "and went straight back down. I'm glad you're getting your story out there, and I hope you find the truth." He hit the table with a clink from his cuffs for added effect. "Do you want me to repeat my story for the documentary? Get me on camera?" He straightened, puffing out his chest.

"No cameras," the lawyer interjected. "We're done here." She motioned to the guard with an agitated head shake.

"Steve, you aren't involved with anyone outside of the prison, right? You aren't telling anyone to do anything illegal, right?" Elise asked in rapid fire. She had to get her questions answered as she fast as she could.

"No way. I'm done with that. Dad manipulated me. You'll hear all about it when we can finally get my appeal in front of a judge. I'm sorry for how I was used. None of it was my idea. I'm a victim, too," Steve said.

The guard hauled him to his feet.

"No more questions, I mean it. My client was taken advantage of and has nothing to do with any other problems. Your town needs a new scapegoat," the lawyer hissed.

She followed Steve and the guard out of the room.

Elise got her feet. She believed Steve, but she didn't like that he wasn't taking responsibility for his actions last summer. Or that he'd given his lawyer the impression he'd been wronged by their town.

"Huh, this didn't turn out the way I expected," Seth said slowly.

"Nor I." She shook her head. "If he's been approached by podcasters, the TV crew would have known about him already. Maybe Kate and Pete really are focused on finding Soupy. I was wrong about the reality TV angle."

"Who destroyed the cameras? Why?"

She shrugged. "Someone playing a prank? Someone who doesn't like to feel that they are living under surveillance?"

"Or someone who knows something they've kept a secret and are worried the cameras will uncover," Seth said.

He was right. What kind of a secret could involve the lake but remain hidden from view of the others? And who would keep such a mystery?

"Sir? Ma'am?" A guard came into the room. "If you'll follow me, please?"

Elise nodded and followed, Seth on her heels. She had a lot to mull over. The TV crew would be back in a few days. They'd have to inform Kate and Pete about what happened.

"I can't believe he never told me about his sighting," Seth said.

"I can." She'd been wrong about Steve, and this piece of news was only one more confirmation of that. Everyone had been wrong about Steve with almost fatal consequences. She'd keep her guard up. Losing control of the narrative had tragic results. She wasn't going to put anyone at risk.

Especially not Seth. She saw now what happened to the gentle souls. Easily led astray or tricked into danger. That wouldn't be Seth's story.

*Chapter Fourteen*

Three days later, Seth twitched his nose, trying not to sneeze as the makeup artist dusted him with powder. The soft bristles of the makeup brush tickled, swishing across his face in broad strokes. Seth fought his instinct to pull back. He didn't want to ruin the handiwork. Even with several interviews under his belt, he hadn't gotten used to the feeling of cosmetics on his skin.

"All set," Tom said and walked away.

"Thanks, Tom," Seth replied with a smile for the artist. Seth's perfectly even skin wasn't the only thing fake at the moment. On the bow of the tour boat, Seth sat in a chair with his back to the water. Everything about the setup was unnatural. He never had his back to the lake. At most, he gave the water his profile so he could always catch movement from at least the corner of his eye.

The arrangement felt more than unusual. It felt vulnerable. Like a betrayal of himself and Soupy somehow. He wished he could send a message to Soupy to pop up behind Seth in the camera's shot to poke fun at this setup.

Pete had insisted on starting with this view of the lake.

Seth had accepted the direction and fell into line without any question. He wasn't one to rock the boat, pun intended, and especially not in light of what happened while the producers were gone, and their curt responses after their return.

The jailhouse meeting had been unexpectedly illuminating. He had never imagined the TV crew was here to do anything besides investigate Soupy. To learn that Elise suspected something else was a shock. No less than Steve revealing he'd encountered Soupy and never said a word.

Seth had always been on edge around Steve. In high school, Seth worried that Elise preferred the other man's company. In an orange jumpsuit, he was—Seth admitted grudgingly—still a handsome guy. Before the events of last summer, Seth had never imagined the secrets he kept. Hearing about a Soupy encounter only solidified that no one had really known Steve.

On the drive back to town, they'd listened to more of the podcast. Seth had no sense of the host's loyalty or reasoning for starting the investigation. A few internet searches pulled up no ties to anyone involved or to Loon Lake. Seth had to accept that the man was seeking to gain fame from other people's suffering.

Seth was glad he had Elise. She had reached out to Kate and Pete, informing them of the camera damage and the police report shortly after the meeting with Steve. To be honest, he'd expected the producers to be in touch long before Elise made the call. The research crew must realize the feeds weren't broadcasting.

Kate and Pete had cut their trip to LA short and returned two days early. They weren't holding any of the property owners liable for the damage. That was good. Seth didn't want to go tit for tat. He held back his comments about the Prims. Neither Hollywood nor Loon Lake was entirely truthful or trusting of the other, it seemed.

Kate and Pete didn't want to waste more time and had moved up all filming schedules. They'd decided to wrap up ASAP. Zach would not be interviewed. Seth figured that was a good punishment for his attention-seeking friend. But that wasn't what bugged Seth.

As far as he knew, the cameras stationed on the lakeshore would not be replaced. If he hadn't worried about the TV crew's intentions before, he was now. Had the decision been made because of financial reasons? Or did they not think they'd capture anything of value on the feeds? They'd come to help uncover the truth. And now it seemed they'd only created more questions.

Seth and Elise had agreed to the new timetable. They were a team. Seth had never been so glad for support as he was now. Whether or not he could count on getting answers to his questions about Soupy, he knew he could depend on her. She remained dedicated to assisting him.

And after? He wanted a proper date and a real chance. Distractions and misdirection flew at him from every turn. But he knew what he wanted.

"Hey," Elise said, approaching from the back. "Are you ready?" She pointed to her collarbone.

He nodded. "Yes, I'm mic'd. Although I think once we get on the water, it'll be hard to hear anything over the wind. How are you?"

She shrugged. "I'm not sure, to be honest."

"If anyone has experience with that, it's me." He chuckled.

She lifted her mouth in a half smile.

"Are you still thinking about the other day?" he asked, careful to remember the recording device attached to his collar and the ears close by. "And...everything?" He had no eloquent way to encapsulate Zach's revelations, and he also had the uneasy sensation that anything he said could be recorded, whether or not he was aware.

"How well do we know anybody, really?" she asked with a shrug but didn't meet his gaze.

*You know me.* He often felt like she was the only person who saw him. In his life, he had the odd sensation of being a sidekick. He listened to Zach's schemes, helped Christopher where possible, and generally chipped in around town. But only Elise ever asked him what he wanted, supported him with the creative partnership for the celebration year, and took his rising status seriously enough to manage him. She saw him.

"Sorry, I didn't mean to get deep and dark this morning," she said, shaking her head.

"What better time and place for reflection than the lake on an overcast day?" He smiled.

She lifted the corner of her mouth. "You always know how to cheer me up. I thought I was supposed to be the coach, managing and encouraging you."

He shrugged. "Why not a give and take?" Movement on the hill near the boathouse grabbed his attention from behind her head.

He stood and walked toward the railing, leaning forward as he squinted. But narrowing his gaze, he wasn't sure what he was seeing.

Mr. Willie stalked across the grass toward the pine forest between the boathouse and the inn. He'd probably been coming back from the Hale Family cemetery, cutting through the boathouse property as a shortcut. That wasn't unusual. Neither was his speed. But the short, jerky motions, the constant turning of his head, and looking behind him.

Was he being followed? Why?

Seth had forgotten about the hooded pair with the camera tracking Mr. Willie. After the discovery of the vandalism, Seth had shifted his attention to that issue. Could the two things be linked? Mr. Willie's stalkers and the vandals? Seth had almost convinced himself they were working for Kate and Pete, but that didn't make sense. Those two being near the damaged equipment implicated them in that crime. After listening to the podcast, he didn't think they worked for Chad Whirl either. If the pair weren't part of the crew, who were they?

Seth wouldn't have thought their town would be on anyone's radar. But that was before he'd learned about the podcaster. *Sins of the Father* predated Seth's fame. How much could he find on a deep dive of the internet? Was Mr. Willie in danger?

Another, perhaps worse, thought slipped into his brain. The stalkers could be the so-called research crew. As far as Seth knew, Mr. Willie was the only person of interest who had refused to appear on camera. The producers were acting cagey. Seth no longer trusted their motives and wondered if they'd decided on their own methods to pursue Mr. Willie and get him on film. Again, he couldn't understand why.

"What's wrong? Do you see something?" Elise asked.

"Elise, do you think that—"

"Good morning," Pete boomed, cutting off Seth midsentence. "Shall we get started? We have a tight schedule today." Pete motioned to the chairs.

Seth glanced at Elise. She looked worried. Did she want to ask him to finish his thought? He wasn't sure he should, not with the microphone on. Pete had saved Seth from potential danger of incrimination. He'd have to follow up with Elise about Mr. Willie later. And maybe he could finally get a chance to speak with the man about his experiences near the water's edge.

If anyone might have seen something suspicious on the water, Mr. Willie would be the prime candidate. And since learning about Steve's encounter that he never shared, Seth questioned whether others had similar stories they hadn't told yet.

"Yes, let's get going. It's perfect weather for Soupy," Seth said.

Pete snapped. "Exactly the enthusiasm I want on camera."

Seth flashed a thumbs-up at Elise.

She shot him a wary look and nodded. "I'll be waiting on the dock when you get back."

He wanted to tell her about his suspicions, but he didn't need an audience. He wanted to insist she stay. But didn't.

There was more than one mystery at Loon Lake. Seth wanted to get to the bottom of them all. One at a time.

* * *

Elise stood on the dock and waved as the boat pulled away, steering into the lake. The plan was to first conduct another interview and then have Seth lead one of his tours, sticking to his script as much as possible. She didn't want to crowd anyone on board, staring over shoulders at monitors and straining to hear what was said over the wind.

Or that was her excuse.

She was afraid she'd get caught on camera in a shot of the lake. Seth was relaxed and comfortable on the screen. This third interview offered another chance to share the same information. Every time, Pete asked a slight variation on the original topics, getting deeper into the why behind Soupy. But Seth didn't need her hovering. He did a great job, and she trusted him.

She had had the sense he wanted to ask her something before Pete interrupted them. She knew Seth would tell her if it was important. He didn't keep secrets. Being partners had taken on a new significance since seeing Steve behind bars.

The visual confirmation of Steve's life as an inmate had

been a wake up to his reality. Until she saw him in his orange jumpsuit, she'd been able to put his circumstances out of her mind. Like when everyone had left for college. He was safe somewhere else.

In truth, he was somewhere else to keep *everyone* safe. He couldn't be trusted. But she couldn't shake that his reaction to news of the filming was genuine. Which only gave her a new problem. If he wasn't behind the vandalism, who was?

Footfalls on the wooden deck behind her snapped her to attention.

She turned and spotted Kate pacing. With her focus on her cell phone, she was in her own world and totally ignorant of the off-beat syncopation her steps made on the wooden dock.

Kate hadn't asked any questions about the damage. She hadn't interrogated anyone about what they'd seen or when they'd noticed or if they had any suspicions. She had accepted the news without comment and taken the police report.

Elise hated not knowing motivations. Why had someone attacked the cameras? And why didn't Kate seem to care about the expensive damage? Were the cameras decoys?

Elise didn't know a lot about technology, but she'd admit the bulky lens on a stick with all sorts of cords hanging off wasn't the sort of high-end gadget she'd expected from a production company. Weren't they supposed to be using Inspector Gadget devices? She had never seen the supposed room being monitored by the science crew. While she was informed of their existence, she hadn't met anyone or been asked to find additional lodging. The converted stables had more than enough space, she supposed. But she wasn't sure about anything, and she hated not knowing specifics.

Grant strolled down the dock, nodding at Kate and stopping next to Elise. "Good morning."

"Hi," Elise said. "Thanks for letting them take the boat out today."

"It's ideal Soupy weather," Grant said with a chuckle. "I can't deny Seth this opportunity."

She wasn't sure if Grant was laughing at or with Seth. As a newcomer, she'd been wary of Grant's intentions from the start. He was a successful tech billionaire who sold his company and retired to their tiny town, buying the Prims' business. He'd had the idea to start the Soupy tours of the lake, the first person to understand the commercial opportunities.

"I'd do anything to support Seth. He's been a good friend," Grant continued.

Elise dropped her crossed arms to her sides but didn't totally let go of her apprehension. "He is a good friend. He deserves the best in return."

Grant arched a brow. "I agree. I'm torn about what I hope the outcome is from the search, to be honest."

"You are?"

"I don't want him to get hurt if they find out Soupy isn't there."

That wasn't her biggest concern, but maybe it should take the top spot.

"Any word about..." he glanced over his shoulder at Kate, "damages," he murmured.

Elise shook her head. "I reached out while they were still in LA. I gave them the police reports in person. Kate thanked me, and that's it. No mention since." She wished she could count on the old cliché about no news. Instead, she waited for the figurative guillotine to drop. Elise's typical approach was to address the problem head-on and ask. But something held her back.

"I don't know if I should be relieved or concerned. I don't like to be kept in the dark."

"Join the club," she muttered.

He chuckled, a full-belly laugh. "How much longer will they be in town?"

"I'm not entirely sure. I'd say at least another two weeks of Kate and Pete," Elise said. She almost mentioned the science crew. She stopped herself. Had she ever seen them? How could she endeavor to make an introduction? She had a lot to consider.

The sound of an engine grew louder, creating ripples in the otherwise still lake as it approached. A hot breeze swept past.

"Hold that thought. I've got to help the team," Grant said.

Elise stayed in place, but Grant positioned himself at the end of the dock to help his crew secure the boat.

"How did it go?" Grant asked when the engine cut and Pete and Seth debarked.

"Great stuff," Pete said.

Seth flashed a thumbs-up.

Elise smiled, a little thrill at his joy.

"Seth was telling me about how you got stranded out on the water," Pete said.

"I did. It was a strange storm." Grant shuddered.

"Did you see anything out there?" Pete asked.

"I couldn't see much of anything in the sheets of rain, but I..." Grant frowned.

"What?" Seth asked.

"Losing command of your vessel, thinking you're at the end of your life, your mind plays tricks on you is all," Grant said. "I don't know that I trust any of my recollection."

"You've never encountered Soupy on the water?" Pete asked, his words crisp and curt.

"Not that I'm aware of," Grant said. "I've only been in business for a year."

Elise held her breath, waiting for the follow-up about the

previous owners. The ones in jail. The bad guys. Why they sold their business.

"We were mostly focused on the treasure hunt on the Timber Triangle," Grant said. "I was too concerned with the curse to worry about Soupy."

Pete's eyes widened at that.

"Curse?" Kate asked.

Elise and the group turned.

Kate had ended her phone call and approached the group in stealth mode.

"The curse nonsense happened in the nineteenth century, the town was very superstitious at the time," Elise said. "A shipment of logs was lost when the sawmill owner, a Maguire, was pushed out of the business, but he saved the crew."

"*A Maguire in possession is prosperity for all*," Grant said.

Elise gritted her molars and held a tight smile.

Loon Lake remained a hotbed for superstitions, but that argument wouldn't help her from her goal of focusing on the search for Soupy and not the slightly unhinged stories of the townsfolk. She did not want to become a roadside attraction: "Come to Loon Lake, where the locals believe in ghosts, cryptids, and curses. Marvel at their gullibility."

"But really, Elise knows all of the lore and legends around here," Grant said. "Don't let me get in her way."

"Elise," Pete said. "We would love to tape your interview today."

"Oh, I don't want to take up your time. I know you have a list of other, more interesting candidates." She forced a laugh.

Pete held her gaze. "You have so much knowledge about the town. You'd add an enlightening angle to the project. What do you say?"

*Nothing could be worse.*

An on-camera interview was her nightmare. When so many of the other interviews had been canceled, she'd hoped hers would be too. But no such luck. She didn't do well being interrogated. She knew her icy demeanor was off-putting to strangers. She'd never sought the limelight or wanted to be part of the story.

She met Seth's gaze, his smile encouraging. Maybe she had to do this to get the documentary on the right track. She'd support Seth. Always. "Okay, let's do an interview."

::: {style="text-align:center"}
## Chapter Fifteen
:::

Seth hadn't realized how much he'd been anticipating this moment—her interview—until it arrived. For much of the last few weeks, he'd been the focus. After his first round of the spotlight thanks to his viral book, he'd adjusted to attention. He'd felt heard for the first time since Dad's passing.

But now he was eager to listen. He wanted to hear what she'd have to say. How long had she been a believer, and what had changed in her heart? Growing up, he hadn't shared about Soupy outside of his family. He didn't fear being teased about his search. But the hunt was too special to share with others.

As an adult, he'd finally felt ready to discuss Soupy. The first time he spoke with Elise about the creature, however, he'd been met with her typical icy stare. She wasn't judging him but testing the strength of his arguments. Slowly, and in her own way, she'd encouraged him. But the change had been so gradual he almost hadn't realized or appreciated when she'd come on board with the Society of Soupy.

When Pete had asked for the interview on the dock, he had

been correct that Elise had insights about the town that only she could share. Seth had spent years listening to her. But he was so distracted by her that he didn't absorb much of what she said. Today, he vowed to actively pay attention.

She looked green.

He frowned.

Sitting on a chair outside the museum, under an overcast sky, the light reflected off nearby trees and made her almost shine from the ambiance.

The makeup artist dabbed at her face with a brush.

Tom didn't have much to do. Elise was the most beautiful woman in town. She shone like a carved stone statue under soft lighting.

Seth waited for Tom to finish the cosmetics before offering up one last pep talk. "Hey." He reached for her hand and squeezed her icy fingers, hoping to instill some warmth. "You're going to be great. The camera will love you. Loon Lake has no better spokesperson than you."

"No," she sighed. "I'm not going to do well. I hate being the center of attention for any amount of time." She squeezed his hand back, staring at their clasped fingers. "I appreciate you lying to cheer me up."

"Not a lie." He pulled his hand free and held up both palms in surrender. "I don't lie. I wouldn't start now."

She met his gaze and nodded. "I know. I'm just... I don't know what to say. What do they want me to talk about? What can I possibly share? How can I add anything of value to your project?"

"It's a conversation. Pete asks questions, and you answer. You're the town historian. Of course you'll have a lot to say. I'll be here the whole time. If you don't know what to say, you can stall. Or make a signal."

"And you'll do what? Run to my rescue?" she asked.

"If that's what you need..." He wouldn't mind the chance

to save her. Elise wasn't a damsel in distress. But he'd like the opportunity to prove himself to her. Maybe this would be his grand romantic gesture.

"I've been thinking about something," she said. "I can't shake that we are missing some obvious part of the puzzle."

"About Soupy?"

"Yes and no." She shrugged. "About the damage specifically. It's easy to pin everything on our original villains. I know it wasn't them. I don't trust Steve, but I believe his sincerity. He committed minor destruction to save his skin."

"But then he aided and abetted a kidnapping," Seth added.

"You're right." She shook her head. "But the camera destruction really hints at desperation, and he has no motive or means."

"I've been thinking too. Whoever committed the vandalism didn't hurt anyone. I don't consider the perpetrator dangerous. They didn't threaten anyone. And nothing has happened since."

"The note was threatening. I worry about escalation though. We missed signs with the Prims. I don't want that to happen again."

Seth understood. As much as he wanted the mystery of Soupy solved, he didn't seek any more danger in town. He'd be glad for their sleepy community to go back to bed.

"I worry about villain decay. That someone is operating at an equally nefarious level as the Prims, but we are desensitized to the danger because of what happened. And, we're on track for something bad. A tragedy of some sort if we don't stop it."

He widened his gaze. He hadn't stopped to consider that they were in danger. Had he done this?

"Elise, we'll get this microphone attached to your sweater and we'll get started, alright?" Pete asked, approaching with the sound tech and doing so without waiting for her definitive confirmation.

"Sure, okay," she said, her voice muffled as the tech clipped the mic in place, standing between Elise and Seth.

"Seth, if you don't mind standing behind the camera?" Pete waved toward the cameraman a few yards off.

"Right, of course," Seth said and took his spot several yards back. He positioned himself to remain in her line of sight, behind Pete's head. If she needed him, she'd have him.

She flashed a thumbs-up.

He nodded, his chest swelling a bit on his next inhale. They were partners. This was his moment to step up for her, and he would.

"Three, two," the camera operator pointed to Pete.

"Elise McKenna is the town's historian. In charge of both the museum and the tourism board, she is a bit of a living encyclopedia of Loon Lake," Pete said.

Her cheeks flushed, and she interlaced her hands in her lap.

"Can you tell us about your town?"

She frowned. "That's a pretty vague question."

Pete chuckled. "Okay, how about what you know of the town's curse, ghost, and cryptid?"

She whitened. She looked like she'd been caught in someone's headlights. "I take it back. I like the vague question."

This time, Pete's laugh was forced and hard. "Why don't you tell us whatever you want us to know?"

She flattened her hands on her thighs. "Loon Lake was originally the site of a lumber operation. The old sawmill, recently restored, was established at the mouth of the channel leading to Lake Superior. In the late nineteenth century, as the timber business was still booming, recreation wasn't top of mind. But Xavier Hale, a businessman from the East Coast, wanted to build a resort. He bought most of the lakeshore for nothing and constructed both his hotel and a boardwalk of shops. No one really lived here at that time. The log cabin that is now our museum was abandoned by trappers some thirty years earlier, after they had felt there was nothing left. Tourism was considered frivolous. But Xavier had a vision, and he was right. The resort became popular, and as the business took off, others flocked to the area to establish their own."

Pete nodded. "Who died to haunt the inn?"

Elise shook her head. "No one. The inn is not haunted. In the early twentieth century, a lighthouse was constructed to claim a small island off the shore of the inn. It was never operational and was built as a folly for guests to enjoy. The current owner of the inn has a very active imagination. Since her childhood, she has claimed to sense spirits on the property. She now suspects her estranged father haunts the lighthouse; he died suddenly, and they never had the chance to reconcile."

"Oh," Pete frowned. "That's sad and sweet."

She nodded and met Seth's gaze.

He gave her another thumbs-up. She was doing great. Why had she been so nervous?

"So, tell us about Soupy."

"I've never seen Soupy," she said.

"Really? You've never seen Soupy?"

"I believe Seth," her voice cracked.

Seth appreciated her unflinching, unhesitating loyalty. But her words had an edge, almost like she was trying to mean what she said. Like she was lying to herself. He shook his head. Elise didn't lie.

"Explain the curse to me," Pete said.

"As the sawmill was nearing the end of its operation, demand waning, the workers were unsatisfied with their diminishing wages. This was the age of the robber barons and unchecked greed. In a bold and thoughtless move, the workers locked the owner out of the mill and took a shipment without him, launching a barge. A sudden storm on Lake Superior struck. The owner could see the lightning from here. He took his personal vessel and rescued the crew after the ship had capsized, valuable cargo sinking to the bottom of the lake. The owner told the crew of a curse that would befall anyone in Loon Lake if one of his line was not in charge of the sawmill."

"No curse, just good propaganda to a very gullible town?"

Seth didn't like Pete's smirk or the smugness. What was wrong with believing in something that couldn't be explained? Who didn't love a good mystery?

"Not every situation in life will have a clear-cut answer," Elise said. "I don't think it's wrong to have questions or to have faith in the unknown or a bigger plan. So no, I have never seen Soupy." She met his gaze again, lifting her chin a little higher. "I believe in Seth."

Warmth spread from the top of his head down to his toes. He had her backing. Maybe he'd never learn the truth about Soupy, and that would be okay. Maybe he didn't need to leave a legacy. Maybe he just had to live a life.

* * *

Elise gripped the thin armrests and adjusted her position.

The elevated director's chairs, with their canvas seats and folding frames, might be easy to move and invisible on screen, but they were awful for real life. She felt like she'd fall. Too high off the ground, she had to rest her feet on a little slat that locked the frame into place. The longer she sat in the canvas, the more she ached and strained the fabric. Would she fall through the chair and land on the ground? Would that make the final cut of the blasted program?

"Let's pause for a second," Kate called. "Pete? Check your messages."

Elise turned toward the voice. The lights focused on her

were blinding, like staring across the lake on a sunny, snowy day. She blinked several times, clearing her vision. She spotted Kate next to the camera operator and the sound technician.

Why was she here? Directing? Elise fought off a shiver. Kate was a far more intimidating foe than Pete.

Pete pulled a phone out of his pocket and quickly became absorbed in the device.

Elise hoped the reprieve would give her a second to gather her thoughts and slow down the interview. She needed to recalibrate somehow and ask him the questions.

"You look great." Kate flashed a thumbs-up.

"You're a natural," Seth called.

Elise smiled at him.

He winked.

Her turn in the spotlight proved just as agitating as she feared. Her voice shook and cracked with every answer. She hated the sound. Her rambling answers weren't helpful. Had she reframed the direct question about Soupy well enough? She didn't want to disappoint Seth or let him down. But she couldn't say—on the record or otherwise—that she believed in something so outlandish as Soupy.

Same with all the other stories locals told. She wanted to show her unequivocal support of the town fantasies with the real facts.

"Let's pick back up," Kate called.

Pete slipped his phone into his pocket and nodded. "As the town tourism manager and the historian for the museum, you have an interesting perspective on the search for Soupy."

"Soupy has been great for the town's visibility. We've had our busiest summer season ever. And it's our sesquicentennial year, so we are delighted to show our town to the world. Loon Lake is a special place. Come discover for yourself."

"That's quite a mouthful," Pete said with a forced chuckle. "Ses-ka-something-able?"

Her cheeks flamed. No one challenged her like Kate and Pete. The producers seemed intent on poking her into a reaction, including teasing her about her work. She wouldn't rise to the bait. "It means one hundred and fifty years. Our town has a very rich history. From the voyageurs, to logging, to tourism, we're constantly adapting to change. We're resilient."

"The town is a special place. I want to talk more about the monster himself," Pete prodded.

She tucked her clammy palms under her legs, readjusting. "I think I've told you everything. You must be pretty sick of my voice. I know I am."

Pete grinned, but something in his expression hardened, his brown eyes turning as hard. "Never. You offer a fascinating glimpse into the town. You must know all of the stories. Are there legends about a monster? A historical record?"

"You must want more than folklore to find the truth."

"You're an expert on the town. You know about the ghost at the Inn at Loon Lake, the Maguire curse, and the Timber Triangle treasure," Pete rattled off the list. "The oral history can be so enlightening to the modern-day."

With each mention, she felt stabs of sharp pain in her stomach. Pete and Kate had deduced that she was the lone skeptic in town. Elise didn't have a poker face and couldn't lie well. She didn't want to get cross-examined about her thoughts and hurt Seth in the process. She had to steer the conversation away from her friends and community. "How is the scientific research going?" she asked, forcing her way onto the topic she was most curious about.

"Oh, it's going," Pete said, cutting his gaze to his notes and then the camera. He shifted in his seat.

With any luck, his breaking the fourth wall would mean they'd end up cutting this whole segment. She almost sighed in relief. Her lifelong micromanaging might have saved her in the end.

"Really? I'd love to hear more about what they are doing. You mentioned taking samples of the lake water. How is that tested? Where's the lab? Are you sending samples somewhere? I'd love to meet the team." She chuckled. "I can't believe I haven't encountered anyone here at the museum. We have an expansive lakeshore. You'd be more than welcome to set up here. I wasn't asked about surveillance, but maybe that would be something fun for visitors to do. I could give them notebooks to make observations."

Pete held her with his gaze.

She didn't move.

He smiled slowly like a predator playing with their prey.

What had she accidentally set up? She gulped.

"We are taking water samples again in a few days. We'd love to include you and take a few from your section of the lake," he said. "Perhaps you and Seth could appear on camera together?"

She darted her gaze towards Seth.

He flashed a double thumbs-up with a huge grin.

She'd agree for his sake. But couldn't ignore the skin-crawling feeling that she was being set up. Would the cameras catch some sort of gotcha moment? Was it a trap?

If she had turned toward Seth even a second earlier, she wouldn't have seen it. Facing Seth and the camera, she spotted movement from the corner of her eye in the general direction of Pete. When she faced her interviewer, she looked past him, narrowing her gaze and squinting. But whatever had been there was gone.

Was it the person responsible for the note about the cameras? What would the assailant think about her ignoring the warning or threat or whatever it was? Setting up with the crew on the grounds of the museum, she acted in defiance of the note. At the present moment, however, she didn't need answers, only escape. She wanted to put on PJs and eat pizza in bed, safe, snug, warm. "Sure, let me know, and we'll accommodate filming."

"Great," Pete said. "Cut. Thanks for doing this. Great stuff." He stood and strode away, barely finishing the platitudes.

The sound tech unclipped the microphone from Elise's sweater.

She carefully stood, not trusting that the chair wouldn't collapse on her as she got away from it. She stretched, her lower body achy and tingly from the uncomfortable seating.

"You were great," Seth said with a smile.

"I was horrible, but thank you for your kind assessment."

He waved off her comment. "You were direct and informative. You've added a lot of gravitas."

Gravitas? She widened her gaze. She wasn't sure she deserved the description and was a little shocked he came up with it.

"I was wondering if you want to get pizza? Celebrate a successful day?" he asked.

She really did. "You've read my mind." She grinned at him, relief flooding her at his reaction. But her curiosity about what she might have seen wouldn't be satisfied by enjoying a meal with her favorite guy. Who was skulking about? Why? "Do you mind if we walk back to town?"

"Sure, perfect weather for it."

And perfect for gathering her thoughts and stalking a mysterious figure. "Let's cut through the woods, come on." She reached for his hand and interlaced their fingers, a zing slipping down her arm at the connection. She wouldn't be brave enough to follow a dark figure into the woods on her own, but she had Seth. Maybe she could have it all, the career, the guy, if she were only gutsy.

*Chapter Sixteen*

For several minutes, Seth didn't speak. He let Elise tug him along at a fast pace, stumbling through the undergrowth of the forest. He felt nothing. He was floating on air.

She held his hand, interlacing their fingers in full view of anyone who might see them and quite a few people who mattered. He hadn't realized how much he'd longed for the validation. She hadn't shied away from their status on their first date at the ice cream shop. But that had been different. That had been in front of Zach, who had known them both forever.

This moment held greater significance. She was bold in front of the cameras. She took hold of his hand like they were an official couple. His moment of triumph was tempered by the understanding that the crew was so busy that no one paid attention to them.

But—it occurred to him slowly—maybe he should try to make sense of their direction. She moved at a clip, with purpose, and not just to get pizza on the boardwalk. This wasn't his romantic gesture time, unfortunately. He wouldn't complain about spending time together as long as he didn't hurt himself in the process.

"Where are we going?" he asked.

"I'm not sure," she murmured. "I saw someone in a hoodie, creeping through the forest, I thought..."

"What?" He stiffened, fear prickling along his spine.

"Maybe it's connected to the cameras and the note? I don't know. I just hate not having answers."

*Hoodie?* He hadn't shared what he'd seen. "Elise, I have to tell you something," he said.

"Later."

"No, now. It's important," he said the words in short bursts. His breathing was shallow.

She frowned at him and slowed her pace, but didn't stop moving. "Okay. I'm listening."

"Do you remember the morning after our all-nighter?"

Her cheeks turned light pink. "I remember."

Hope flared in his chest at her reaction. He hadn't missed his chance at being more than friends yet. He'd throw a rock through the window of opportunity if he had to to keep it open.

But right now, he needed to focus. "Right. Great. When I dropped off the issues at the inn, I spotted Mr. Willie heading out through the forest. It occurred to me that no one knows this area like him. And he hasn't ever said more than a few words to me. I figured he must know something, so I followed him."

"Like we're doing now," she murmured.

"I wasn't the only one. There were two people with a professional-looking camera chasing after him, too. At the time, it really bugged me. I can't figure out who they might be. Before I could do anything, I got the group text. Then everything happened during the meeting at the inn with the cameras being damaged and Zach and the podcast. It slipped my mind until today. I was getting ready to get on the boat, and I saw him. What if he's in danger? What if we're in danger by following this person into the woods?"

In the thickest part of the woods, they reached a fallen log.

She dropped her hold of his hand and climbed over the timber with ease. "Let's be careful and quiet. Too late to turn around now."

He straddled the log and swung his leg over, hopping to the other side. "Shh, listen," he whispered, straining.

She widened her gaze and tipped her head to the right.

He nodded. Glad she'd heard it too. A faint sound that could be the wind rustling leaves or flowing water. He hadn't explored this part of the forest surrounding the museum, boathouse, and Hale family cemetery. If he had business at the boathouse or the museum, he drove. Cemeteries freaked him out.

He had his reasons, but logically, he had a hard time digesting that part of the landscape had been unknown to him. Did part of the lake extend here? Was there some sort of pond connected with an underground cave to the lake? Nothing about the topography would surprise him. Glaciers had carved massive caves on the Apostle Islands just north of the channel. His search for Soupy hadn't been as exhaustive as he'd previously thought.

On tiptoes, he followed Elise, careful to step where she had, avoiding branches, twigs, and limbs. He didn't want to make excessive noise or step into a hole and twist his ankle. While he hadn't spotted any danger, he couldn't deny the charge in the air. The unknown beckoned.

They reached another fallen tree, and the scent of freshwater, mud mixed with reeds, and something rotten overwhelmed him. A few yards off, he spotted a hooded figure kneeling at what must be the water's edge.

He pulled her to crouch behind the log. He didn't think

they were in danger, per se, but the figure didn't want company. What was the person doing? Who was it?

"Just a few more days," a deep voice cooed, carrying on the wind.

Water lapped and splashed.

Seth knew that voice. Why was Mr. Willie here? A sharp elbow hit his ribs.

"Mr. Willie?" she mouthed.

Seth shrugged. If anyone would know about a secret spot, it would be the inn's groundskeeper. But again, why?

"I'll come back soon, my sweet. Stay low," Mr. Willie said.

His voice was soft, almost a coo. Like the way some people spoke to their pets. That couldn't be right. Why would Mr. Willie keep an animal out here? Why not at the inn? The Lewises might have restrictions about pets inside the inn, but they wouldn't be cold-hearted about the caretaker cottages on their property, housing their longest-tenant, the ever-loyal Mr. Willie.

Branches snapped and crunched as Mr. Willie strode away.

Elise started to rise, but Seth stopped her, pulling her down with a gentle tug. She slid into him, landing against his chest. She looked up at him slowly through her lashes.

His heartbeat thundered in his ears. If Mr. Willie had returned, he'd find them. Seth didn't care. He'd never been so close to Elise before. With such microscopic inspection, she was even more perfect than from afar. Her skin glowed. Her full lips parted, and her tongue darted against her lower lip.

This was the moment. He could kiss her. Should he? Did she want him to? Maybe this wasn't very romantic. But he was tired of waiting for perfect conditions. He swallowed the lump in his throat.

And she moved away, standing and dusting her hands on her legs before striding away, around the log.

Was she disappointed? Had she wanted him to make a move? Had he screwed everything up?

"Seth, did you see something in that water?" she asked.

He scrambled to his feet and approached.

The water thrashed, bubbles popping at the surface. And then the water was silent and deep. A hot spring? Some sort of connection to the lake? He bent and dipped his hand into the water. The temperature was as cold as the lake, around fifty-eight degrees. There must be an underground tunnel leading from the spot to the shore.

He stood, drying his hands on his pants, and examined the shape. The irregularity didn't look manmade, and there would be no purpose in building a little pond out here. It was too small to launch any watercraft, and he couldn't see any fish.

"Do you see any signs of...anything?" she asked. "Animal? Mineral? Vegetable?"

She sounded frantic. She was grasping at anything to make sense of what they'd sort of seen. Seth had no answers for her and no way to make sense of the odd behavior they'd witnessed or the mystery of the brand-new location.

"What is this place?" Seth asked. "Does it belong to the cabin?"

She nodded. "Yes, and don't get too near that water or put your hand in again. This was the rudimentary sewer system for the cabin. The smell has been enough to keep me away. I never wanted to know what might be found here."

*Like fossilized... droppings?* He recoiled.

"Now I'm wondering if the smell isn't entirely natural but intentional to discourage visitors."

"We need to talk to Mr. Willie," Seth said slowly, a plan forming. "Find out what he's up to and what he knows. He's involved with something." Seth couldn't begin to fathom what. Had Mr. Willie gotten involved with bad people who were out for vengeance? Was he being blackmailed? Why?

"No, you should do that," she said, interrupting his runaway train of thought. "I want to talk to Kate and Pete. I'm tired of waiting. I want action."

Did she just mean about the project? Or did she include him? "Okay. I'll go find him."

"Raincheck for dinner?" he asked.

She nodded and strode away.

He watched her disappear in the direction of the museum, and then he slowly followed the way Mr. Willie had gone. Maybe Seth would first get answers from the elusive groundskeeper and then he'd go in search of more for himself. He had to get direct. He could do this. He had to.

* * *

He was just so darn sweet and nice.

Elise groaned as she stormed off, back to the museum. She knew he would never kiss her without expressly given consent. She loved that about him. But also? Right now? When she really wanted to kiss him, but he pulled away, she wished for a second he wasn't so nice. If he was sparing her feelings, he should just tell her. She felt like a fool and like she'd wasted the last opportunity she'd ever be given to change their friendship to a romance.

Maybe he read the signs of her attraction and turned her down. This time, she hadn't tried to stop him by speaking. She'd kept her mouth shut or, more accurately, slightly parted. But she hadn't said anything. Her skin burned from his nearness and now chilled from the distance. Frustration bubbled up in her throat. This was exactly why she ignored feelings. The horrible, out-of-control emotions clouded every interaction and complicated everything. What should have been easy —helping Seth and protecting the town—had become a hopeless tangle of gossip, crime, and humiliation.

And she was no closer to achieving her goals. She'd been swamped with trying to stay ahead of litigation and hadn't checked the online accounts or started the mailing for her funding drive or anything. Her phone rang in her pocket.

She pulled out the cell and stared at the screen. The mayor had called.

"Ugh. Not now," she mumbled, silencing the device and slipping it back in her pocket.

She pounded the ground under her feet, retracing her steps. The pine needles softened the sound of her progress. As she neared, she realized that no one had noticed her disappearance.

The crew hadn't finished dismantling the setup. They were still lowering lights, collapsing chairs, and wrapping and storing cords.

Despite her not-so-subtle stomping, no one spared her a glance. Fine. A surprise entrance suited her purpose.

In her pocket, her phone shook from another incoming call. Whatever Tim had to say could wait. She was on a mission. She rounded the side of the log cabin and spotted Kate and Pete.

Sharing a pair of headphones, they stared at a screen.

She narrowed her gaze, focusing on the images as she neared.

Snippets of the race, the parade, cardboard Soupy floating away and sinking, she was watching outtakes like one might see late at night on TV. But the faces weren't anonymous. They were familiar. Her friends. Her town. Good people she had known forever were now laughingstocks. Her skin burned from embarrassment, frustration, and rage. The town trusted her, and she'd let them all down.

The images on the screen were worse than a reality show. Loon Lake became a punchline. It was a reduction of their town into slapstick. Were the producers listening to some cutting voice-over narration? Or worse, canned laughter?

"What is that?" Elise barked, holding out a shaky finger to the screen.

Kate and Pete jumped, dropping the headphones and unplugging from the screen. False laughter rang out. Kate stopped the playback.

"Oh, hi, Elise," Pete said.

"How can we help you?" Kate asked.

"What are you doing? What was that video?" Elise asked, her limbs trembling. She locked her knees. She wouldn't crumble.

"Just an idea," Kate said and shrugged. "Another potential avenue."

"You are here to help Seth find Soupy," Elise said.

"We are," Pete agreed.

"So why are you making fun of our town? What does that have to do with the project?" Elise asked, her voice cracking. She was fragile and vulnerable. She hated it. She had never felt so exposed and used. Where did she place the blame?

"We have to explore all sorts of options to recoup our investment. It's just business," Kate said. "Nothing personal."

Elise scoffed. Nothing personal? The producers had insisted on interviewing her only moments ago. What was the point? To make her feel insecure and hold her down? All the while, they had been piecing together a terrible blooper reel. Their edited footage would ruin the town and have far-reaching consequences for the future of everyone in Loon Lake. Tourism—the major industry—would dry up, and then what would happen? "You said you would wrap up filming soon. Why? Because you've given up?"

"We are following several leads," Pete added.

Elise didn't want excuses. She was hungry, tired, and heart-broken. Why would she believe this pair after what she'd just watched on the screen over their shoulders, when they thought she wasn't around? "No. You're not. If you were, you'd be here for longer. You don't have the answers you need."

"We don't have the answers you want," Kate said, tapping a finger to her chin. "That's not the same thing as not having a solution."

"What's your solution? Sell a series of funny videos of mishaps? That you caused?" Elise asked.

"What are you talking about?" Pete asked, narrowing his gaze.

"Be very careful," Kate advised. "You'd hate to say something that couldn't be taken back or that could be considered slander."

Elise let out a bark of laughter. Now the producers had a backbone. Verbal combat brought out their legal team? They had wanted to ignore the damage to their equipment but wouldn't stand for a bad word. She couldn't make sense of it.

In her pocket, her phone buzzed again. She pulled out her cell, glad for the device to give her a distraction and a moment to catch her thoughts. Four missed calls from Tim flashed on the screen. And a voicemail.

She gulped. She probably owed him an accounting of what had happened at the jail with Steve Prim. He'd asked to be kept in the loop. She really had no way of explaining her biggest failing of all, letting down Seth and ruining the town's image. No, she'd fight back for Seth's sake and hers. She had too much to do to let a couple of bad actors prey on the town.

"What about the supposed research crew?" Elise asked.

"Nothing supposed about them," Kate replied. "In fact, we are heading to film them right now, if you'd like to join us."

"Film them doing what?" Elise asked.

"Maybe you'd like to see," Pete said.

His smile was smooth as ever. Elise shuddered. While she'd

been worried about one angle, she hadn't stopped to consider another. Being caught unawares was the problem she'd feared from the start. By dropping her guard, she'd disappointed everyone. Seth pulled away, and that was the smart choice. She couldn't keep him safe if she let her emotions take charge.

She'd lean into the science and get the answers they all needed. She'd be fine with the status quo.

*Chapter Seventeen*

For a man in his late sixties, John Willie was surprisingly spry. And agile. Seth jogged after him from the small pond or creek or whatever it was and up the hill leading to the Hale family plot. At the top, he had to stop and catch his breath. With both hands on his waist, he bent over almost completely, dragging in every ounce of air he could. When he lifted his weary gaze, however, he spotted nothing.

Mr. Willie hadn't slowed to catch his breath. Add marathon athlete to the list of secret skills the man possessed. After a lifetime in town, Seth had never realized how little he knew about any of his neighbors. He accepted what he was presented, not pressing harder or deeper to learn about each individual. Mr. Willie was more myth than man, and that had never bothered Seth until today.

Seth raced down the hill toward the inn. Had Mr. Willie gone back to the hotel? Or to his house? Where did he live? Was this a bad idea? Was he in danger? Was Seth now in trouble?

Trekking into the pine forest, Seth's foot caught on an

exposed root. "AAHH," he squealed as he flew in midair and crashed to the ground.

Everything hurt. He held still, struggling to take in a breath as he assessed the physical damage. He tasted blood in his mouth. He must have bit his lip. His head ached. His ankle hurt, but he could rotate the joint. He opened his mouth and moaned, just to see if he could make a noise. He could do that. Bruises were the extent of the damage.

"Lad! What are you doing?" John Willie asked.

Heavy footsteps drew near, shuffling on the pine needle-covered ground.

"Ugh," Seth groaned. With a hand, he pushed himself over until he rolled onto his back.

Mr. Willie bent and extended a hand. "Are you alright? Can you get up?"

"Maybe," Seth said. He accepted Mr. Willie's hand and let himself be hauled to his feet. His head pounded, and the world spun. He leaned against a nearby tree.

"What were you doing? You know better than to race into the woods."

"What were *you* doing?" Seth asked, turning the question back on him. He probably should have come up with a better way to get to the point. A cleverer turn of phrase. But he'd never been accused of wit and couldn't find any now.

Mr. Willie crossed his arms. "Were you following me?"

"Yes," Seth replied, slight exasperation coloring his tone.

Mr. Willie drew back his chin.

In Seth's experience, most of the time, people were thrown off by the truthful answer when asked a direct question. But that moment of victory wouldn't stop him from pushing ahead. "What do you keep in that little pond?"

"Does anyone else know about it?" Mr. Willie darted his gaze. "Were you followed? Did you tell anyone?"

"Elise knows about the pond because she's the caretaker

for the cabin. We both saw you. We followed you. If you see something, say something, right?"

Mr. Willie stroked his chin. "And she'd be thorough enough to conduct a survey of the plot of her land."

He sounded impressed but didn't answer any of the questions swirling in Seth's mind. What could be lurking just under the surface, and why the secrecy? "Mr. Willie, I've never asked you if you've had any encounters with anything out of the ordinary in the lake."

"No, you haven't. But I'm not much of a person around here. I'm part of the institution of the place."

The words were almost cutting. No one had suspected Carl and Steve Prim of misdeeds. Their lawyer, Leonard Baird, had also been overlooked. Now all three were behind bars for a host of criminal charges aimed at both property and persons. Had Mr. Willie been part of their ilk? Were there more? For everyone's sake, Seth wanted an explanation that wasn't unlawful.

"Mr. Willie, you've always been one of the grown-ups to me. You still are. I hadn't asked you about Soupy before because I didn't want to bother you. I figured you would tell me if you knew anything. I've made my project no secret."

Mr. Willie shifted his weight from one foot to the other.

"Have you ever had an encounter you can't explain?"

Mr. Willie shook his head.

Seth's stomach dropped to his feet. He'd really been hoping Mr. Willie had the answers he needed. "So, you have an answer for every situation?"

Mr. Willie nodded.

"What was in that pond? I heard you talking like it was a p—"

"Great, you're both here," Pete called, panting.

Seth whirled around, nearly tripping over his feet again. He spotted Elise in the group, squinting against the bright light on the front of the camera. The entire crew barreled towards Seth and Mr. Willie, boom waving out in front like a carrot before a horse in an old cartoon.

Elise made a circular motion.

*Filming? This? Why?*

"Hi, Pete. I thought we were done for the day?" Seth asked, hopeful he could get away from the crew and get answers.

"We were, but the reports came back. I wanted both of your reactions on film," Pete said.

"Reports?" Mr. Willie asked, rubbing his hands together.

"Us?" Seth waved between himself and Mr. Willie.

"Yes, the two most important people for the documentary," Pete said. "After all, Mr. Willie sabotaged the cameras and has been misdirecting the research from the start."

"You have?" Seth frowned and sucked in a breath. Moving the muscles in his face hurt. He reached up a hand and felt a goose egg on the top of his forehead in his hairline. He winced.

Elise cut through the crowd, justling the cameraman to reach his side. She leaned close, holding his face in her hands. "Are you okay? What happened?"

"He took a spill," Mr. Willie replied. "Chasing after me. And I've had enough of your accusations." Mr. Willie waggled a finger at the TV host. "You don't belong here. You've done more harm than good. Leave our town alone."

"I have evidence of your subterfuge, Mr. Willie. Believe me, if I wanted, I could press charges and sue for damages. But what I want, instead, is answers for the town and for Seth," Pete said, raising his chin.

He had a flair for the dramatic. Seth would give him that. "What do you mean?"

Pete pulled a white envelope out of his back pocket and held it in the air, dangling it between his fingers. "I received the results of our DNA analysis of the lake." He slipped a folded sheet of paper out of the already open envelope. "While we found the expected amounts of fish, dogs, and humans, we were stunned to learn of 5 percent DNA consistent with a Greenland shark."

A Greenland shark? What on earth was that? "I don't follow. Something else is in the water with Soupy?"

"Well, there was 10 percent unknown, that could be anything." Pete waved a hand. "But a Greenland shark in these waters is a rare occurrence. They would not typically be found here. They can live for hundreds of years and are prehistoric. This is a major discovery."

Seth didn't like the quick, curt dismissal. "But it's not a mosasaurus."

Pete shot him a pitying look. "Correct."

*So what?* Seth wanted to counter. The lake was large enough for an underwater world of secrets. But as Pete continued to stare him down, Seth became hyper-aware of everyone's gaze, laser-focused on him. Including the camera. "You think this shark is Soupy? How would it have found its way into the lake?"

"Someone must have brought it here," Pete said. "Isn't that right, Mr. Willie?"

Mr. Willie flinched.

"What?" Elise gasped. "Mr. Willie? You were behind the vandalism? You brought an invasive species to the lake?"

"He's not invasive if he has no partner. There is no unlawful breeding happening. He was my pet, but he grew too big for his tank. I had no choice," Mr. Willie said. "Patrick isn't a danger to anyone."

"We won't press charges if you agree to an on-air interview and explanation," Pete said. "I'll be honest, when I arrived, I didn't think I'd find a neat ending for this narrative." Pete clapped a hand on Seth's shoulder. "But I was wrong. We did it! You should be thrilled. Go and celebrate."

Seth felt...nothing. Soupy was real. But he wasn't a mosasaurus. And Mr. Willie had known the truth the entire time. Years of researching and chasing after someone's overgrown pet? Seth had let down everyone in town. The Society of Soupy wouldn't love a Greenland shark. They wanted a real living dinosaur with sharp teeth in a terrifying jaw.

More importantly, he'd ruined the legacy he was supposed to be building for his family. Instead of their names in history for a great find, they'd be relegated to a curious footnote about a ridiculous idea. What he'd done to establish them would ultimately be his ruin. How could he face Mom and Lauren with the news? His blood ran ice cold, clogging in his veins.

"You did it! You made a real discovery. I can't believe this. This is the best news," Elise said, wrapping her arms around him and squeezing.

He should have felt something then, right? Her enthusiasm had never been more effusive. Her touch was warm and welcoming. She leaned close, like she wanted a kiss. But all he felt was the cold fingers of dread. Because it seemed like everyone was in on the stunt except for him. Was he the town fool? And worse, did she pity him, too?

* * *

In one moment, Elise's worst fears were realized, and in the very next second, the best outcome was achieved. The TV crew had intended to curate their footage into a blooper reel about Loon Lake. They never intended to help Seth. And they had decided that instead of the heartwarming angle of the father-and-son adventure that had put their town on the map, they'd make everyone a joke.

After last summer's devastating betrayals, Loon Lake

wouldn't survive Kate and Pete's interpretation of the town. As her worries multiplied by the second, however, she didn't see the rescue happening in real time. Against all odds, however, Seth had been right. Finding Soupy saved them all.

She couldn't believe her good fortune. Crisis averted. Times a thousand. Why didn't Seth look happy? He'd been right! Against all odds, a creature lurked in Loon Lake, and its identification was a major story.

Seth was quiet. Almost stony in his silence. She would have prodded him with an elbow if she wasn't concerned about his fall. Was he in shock? Should she take him to the hospital to be checked for a concussion? Was he suffering internal bruising?

She leaned close. "Hey, Seth. Talk to me. Are you feeling okay? Do you want to go to the hospital to get checked out?"

His pupils weren't dilated and, as far as she could tell, he had normal brain function.

He shook his head.

"You should be jumping up and down," she continued. "This is great news. You made a huge discovery. Your stories are now verified." She grabbed him by the shoulders and squeezed. "You aren't making up stuff. You're a big deal."

He stiffened and shook off her touch, turning his back and walking away. Stalking off in the opposite direction. In the second before he'd turned, his gaze had darkened, losing the usual warmth in his green eyes. He'd gone cold. Under her fingers, he'd been like ice.

"Do you suppose Mr. Willie blackmailed Zach? How did he get those photos?" She shuddered. The images that threatened Zach were personal and private. How had the groundskeeper come into possession of them? She never would have suspected him. At least she could comfort herself that this time, murder and mayhem hadn't been on the villain's radar. She really wasn't sure how to classify Mr. Willie. Concerned pet owner?

"Maybe the older ladies were air-dropping indiscriminately amongst each other," Seth said. His voice was flat. Dead. Distant.

She had to focus on him. She wasn't doing a very good job of managing if she ignored him.

He wasn't close. He stalked off, no stopping.

She narrowed her gaze, scanning the tree line. He'd made quick work of getting away from her. No, not from her. From a tense situation. He needed space to process all the news. She hoped. In a way, she'd been right with her own theory the entire time. Soupy was a pet. But she didn't want to take away from his moment with her own victory.

She carefully made her way through the trees, picking up her feet with each step to avoid any tree roots. She found him on the edge of the forest and the inn, near the neatly trimmed row of boxwoods marking the perimeter of the manicured grass. "Hey," she huffed and puffed. "Stop. What's wrong? Let's chat."

"Why?" He crossed his arms over his chest.

"What do you mean? Because I understand that you must be feeling overwhelmed by all of this. Tell me what's going on in your head."

"Nothing. Right? I'm just the silly, stupid town fool. Right?" His words hissed, threatening a venomous bite.

She flinched.

"You think I invented Soupy. You think I'm an idiot."

She shook her head. "I think you have had experiences on the water that led you to a conclusion that wasn't bolstered by facts or science."

He rolled his eyes.

"But I was wrong," she pleaded. "There was a monster in the lake after all. You've made an amazing discovery."

"No, that thing isn't Soupy. I've never seen that creature before. And Soupy isn't a domesticated pet." He pinched the bridge of his nose. "He wouldn't come when called and couldn't fit into that little creek. Besides, the timeline doesn't match. The first time I saw Soupy, Mr. Willie wasn't here yet. I don't think... I'm not sure... None of this adds up."

She gritted her molars, curling her fingers into fists at her sides and slowly releasing a breath. "How on earth can you believe it's really a mosasaurus?" Her tone was sharp. She wanted a softer delivery, but she was incredulous. She didn't want to hurt his feelings, but she couldn't back down. The discovery was remarkable. He'd be part of the town's history forever, like he wanted.

His green eyes looked more like dull moss than brilliant emeralds.

"Come on, Seth," she murmured, stepping close. "What you're saying doesn't make sense. It doesn't mean I don't support you, just because I can't suspend logic. This is the best outcome for everyone. The Greenland shark will give the TV crew an answer and a way to package the program. They'll go home, and we can all get back to our lives."

"Can we?" He narrowed his gaze.

This time, she stiffened.

"Tell me, what is my life? What they found isn't the Soupy that I've been selling. So I'm a fraud at best. And at worst?" He shrugged. "I'm a joke. The slapstick comedian to your straight man persona. You've been laughing at me the whole time."

Her blood chilled in her veins. She crossed her arms over her chest and shook her head. "No, never. I think you're a dreamer. Maybe a little gullible. But not a joke."

"And I think you can be cold and calculating."

She sucked in a sharp breath. Sure, she'd heard those throwaway jibes over the years in one form or another. With each insult, she'd added another block of ice to the wall between herself and the rest of the world. But she'd never imagined he'd say it. Seth might be the only person she'd ever let see her soft and warm. Now, he was a stranger. "Maybe this is a mistake," she murmured, staring at the ground.

"Why? Because you can't control me after all? Because you pity me?"

She shook her head.

"Either you are worried about what others think, or those are your opinions about me. And both choices suck. If you actually cared for me, you wouldn't focus on public opinion. I don't care what people say."

"That's because you're brave."

He scoffed. "Or stupid."

"If you won't listen to me, you owe yourself a call with your family."

"You don't get it." He hung his head. "Goodbye, Elise."

She nodded but didn't watch him go. It would hurt too much. Besides, whether she wanted to or not, she had work to do on his behalf. She never reneged on her contractual agreements. Even when her heart was snapping in half. She'd have to discuss setting up the interview with Mr. Willie and getting them to put in writing that they wouldn't press charges against him. Someone would need to contact scientists, real marine biologists, to learn what to do about the shark.

The DNR would have opinions. Fish and wildlife would, too. Many departments would have an interest in the lake at the local, state, and federal levels. Mr. Willie would have a lot to explain and potentially defend against litigation.

The convoluted chaos was like the debris left after the lighthouse's explosion last year. Everyone would have been better off if nothing had been messed with. If she was lucky, she could wrap this all up today. She could get the TV crew and the whole program mess out of her life. And then she could cry herself to sleep.

She rubbed her palms together and blew hot air on her hands. The chill was unexpected on the warm day. She glanced at Pete, Mr. Willie, and the TV crew.

The small group was focused on their own conversation. Elise needed to stay and be part of it. Mr. Willie had vandalized the cameras. Or he'd been responsible.

# Chapter Eighteen

Seth didn't have a destination in mind. He'd never stormed off before. In his entire, admittedly blessed, life, he hadn't felt such ire rising in him, clouding his brain and fogging his vision with a red haze. The landscape blurred, and he was only aware of the thundering heartbeat in his ears and the way the ground remained solid and immovable under his feet. He wouldn't leave a trace of himself behind. Fitting.

Did he head home? Go to the ice cream shop? Jump in the lake to cool off? The deep, dark water would barely register his presence. He'd slip under the surface without much disturbance.

"Whoa, where are you off to?" Ashley called.

Seth stopped and raised his gaze, taking in his surroundings. He'd made it through the forest and across the front of the inn toward the old stables.

"Hey, Seth? Is everything alright?" she asked, drawing nearer.

Dressed in paint-splattered jeans and an oversized sweatshirt, she was a far cry from the sophisticated influencer she'd been when she first returned to town.

"Do you need a drink of water?" She neared and sucked in a sharp breath. "Ouch, what happened to your head?"

"Huh?" He frowned at her and touched his crown. A dull ache throbbed under raised flesh. "Oh, I tripped."

"Come inside, I'm touching up the paint in the guest rooms. I have some water and aspirin. You can take a rest and tell me what's going on."

He didn't fight off her touch on his elbow, tugging him into the half of the stables rented out to guests. The smell of wet paint poured through the open windows and door. After a second, however, he didn't notice it anymore. He was glad to be inside, in the shade, and out of view.

She pointed to a chair in the kitchenette and left the room.

He sank into the seat, grateful for the support. He needed grounding of any kind at the moment. He'd either fly away or sink into the bottom of the lake.

When Ashley returned, she handed him a lukewarm bottle of water and a jar of pills. He accepted both, grateful for the concern. Elise had been concerned, too. Why wouldn't she be? He was her little pet. Never her equal. Not someone she could build a life and partnership with. No, he was someone to manage. Another annoying and sometimes accidentally comedic item on her list to be handled.

"Why are you painting? Isn't that someone else's job?" he asked. He read the package's directions and swallowed two pills, chasing them with a sip of the water.

"Probably. But I like to get my hands dirty. The film crew moved into the other side of the cottage, so Christopher and I got our home back."

"Did they wreck it? Leave it a mess?"

She shook her head. "No. I needed a change."

She said the words slowly, like she wasn't telling him everything. Like another reason lurked behind the façade of a fresh start. Like everyone else had been hiding something lately. He was tired of that. Not that Ashley needed to explain herself to him. Of all the people in town, she'd always been upfront and honest, never keeping a secret. She owed him nothing.

"What's going on?" Ashley asked, taking the other chair and resting an arm on the small bistro table. "What's wrong? We're friends. You can tell me."

He took a gulp of water and pushed down every feeling now bobbing in his dry, scratchy throat. He didn't want to cry while he spoke. But he didn't know how to separate his emotions from the situation. Maybe that was the biggest problem for Elise. He would always be a liability to a person who craved order. "I tripped in the forest chasing after Mr. Willie."

"Okay, so that's your physical injuries. Why are you so upset?"

"Soupy is real."

"We knew that."

Hearing those words, so matter-of-factly, warmed him. She didn't sound condescending or skeptical. She accepted him. Too bad the only person he wanted such treatment from couldn't give it. "I don't think everyone did. Soupy is actually Mr. Willie's pet named Patrick. He's been feeding him and taking care of him for years."

"Really? That's incredible. I never thought of Mr. Willie as a pet person."

"Neither did I. But we know the truth now."

"Wow," Ashley said. "You have definitive proof that she, or he, I suppose, exists. *The truth always surfaces.* Just like you said. Wonderful news."

"In the wrong place and the wrong species," he murmured. Everything he had said about Soupy for decades was proved incorrect. Did that make him a fool or a liar? He wasn't sure which option was worse.

"Not on the open water?" Ashley asked.

He shook his head.

"How can they be sure Patrick is Soupy? How do they explain Molly and Grant's encounter last summer?"

Seth shrugged. "I suppose they don't. Or it'll be suggested that one of the timbers was loose and rammed the boat." He appreciated Ashley's continued acceptance of his version of the lake monster. "Can I ask about...the ghost?"

"Of course." She nodded and leaned back. "Anything you want to know."

"When you first came back, you were faking being a ghost, right?"

She nodded, her expression serene and utterly nonplused.

"But then, it became real?"

"Yes. The strange occurrences I had were too inexplicable to be anything else. My dad was reaching out to me from the other side. I haven't sensed anything now in the rebuilt lighthouse. But I'm still comforted by what happened last summer."

He wished he could be as calmly confident. The reverse had happened to him. He'd known Soupy was real. For decades, his belief was enough to sustain him. But now, learning the monster wasn't what he had expected, he was deflated. And the one person he'd needed to understand and get his mixed feelings had been so relieved that he wasn't an idiot, she told him he was a fool.

"I still can't get over Mr. Willie caring about a living creature and nurturing it," she said, her voice full of wonder. "How long has Mr. Willie had the pet?"

Seth appreciated that the most unbelievable part of the whole circumstance to Ashley was the revelation of someone's character, and not Seth's failure. "Apparently, Mr. Willie brought Patrick to the inn when he first started. It's a Greenland shark. Once it grew too large for a tank, he released the shark into the lake. That's what I've been seeing all these years."

"Really?" She stroked her chin. "Huh. From your first-hand accounts, I really thought it was a mosasaurus."

"Me too." Seth sighed. "But as I was confronting Mr. Willie, the TV crew was on their way with the results of the DNA test of the water that corroborate the presence of a Greenland shark. My Soupy wasn't real."

"I don't think that's accurate. Your Soupy has done a lot of good for this town. That's been real. What does Elise say?"

"That she's relieved they found it."

"Hmm, she was worried about Loon Lake becoming the punchline for late-night TV hosts."

He didn't blame her for that. She did work hard, running multiple sectors for the town that each should have been staffed by at least three people. The community was her number one priority. He could kind of see what she was getting at with being glad they could wrap up the narrative neatly. "Can I...share something? Personal?"

"Of course."

He blew out a sigh and stared at his interlaced fingers on the tabletop. "This isn't what I wanted, and it's definitely not what I needed to leave a mark in our town's story. You might not understand. You're part of a legacy family. I'm just part of the nameless population. But Dad..." He shut his eyes tight against the tears. "Dad deserved more. I don't want him to be forgotten."

"I'm sorry that it didn't work out the way you'd hoped." Ashley rested a hand on top of his.

He opened his eyes and met her gaze.

"But legacy isn't all it's cracked up to be. I grew up in a shadow that I was never able to escape. I wouldn't want that for anyone. No one who was blessed to know your father will ever forget him. Maybe that's more important than being entombed in a textbook with a couple sentences." She squeezed his hand. "You had one person who fully believed in you. And you have another who wants to be there for you. That's pretty lucky. Maybe you don't need more."

Maybe Ashley was right. Loving Elise meant he'd always come up against her rational, logical, analytical side. That's who she was. And he valued and respected her caution and care. But she didn't return his affection. He was an obstacle, a distraction, a side show. He wasn't the main event.

"I for one," Ashley continued, "am keeping my Society of Soupy merchandise and will consider the hunt to still be on. The lake is deep and dark. Plenty of space for a few mysteries. Remember, the truth always surfaces."

Did it? He lifted his gaze but stared unseeing. There was a portion of DNA in the lake that remained unidentifiable. He wouldn't give up on Soupy or Dad. He owed everyone more of a fight. "Thanks, Ashley. I've got some work to do."

* * *

Watching someone walk away was tough. Letting Seth leave was Elise's only option. Exerting power wasn't the right path. Blocking his path and fighting him would get her nowhere. But she hated feeling like a bystander to her own life as the most important person in it stormed off. She folded her arms over her chest and gripped her biceps tightly. She'd have a bruise in the morning. Better that than collapsing in an emotional heap on the ground.

She hated being a victim or a martyr. She handled things. She was the boss. If she stepped on toes in the process, she could apologize later. Only now she worried she had turned into a bully. In her attempt to mitigate feelings, she'd crushed him. And snapped her heart in two in the process.

She wasn't the running-after-him, grand-gesture type of

person. He made it pretty clear he wanted space. She didn't blame him. She wanted a break from herself, too. All she wanted was to protect him. Every action she took was in pursuit of that goal.

Except... Maybe her words proved that she valued her public persona more than his heart. She exhaled a heavy sigh. With high school long behind her, she shouldn't care what anyone thought about her. And she didn't value her image more than him.

But more than that, she'd let him down. Seth deserved her full encouragement, especially when it was hard to do. She believed in him. Her faith had never wavered. Seth was remarkable. She hated that he didn't see what an impact he'd had on all those around him.

Who cared about one line in a textbook? He was a living legend and would become part of the oral history of their community. If she could just shake him loose from the idea that Soupy could only be an extinct sea creature, she had a chance. He wouldn't budge on that classification. She would support him. But would he speak to her again?

What could she do? *Make amends.* The documentary makers had their answer. But they'd almost admitted their science was more consequences than an actual search for the truth. Perhaps they'd add in an angle to leave the mystery open-ended.

She marched over to the crew and tapped Pete on the shoulder until he spun around. "Show me what you have."

"Excuse me?" He dropped his smirk and narrowed his gaze.

"I said what I said. You have not been honest. Your whole project has been filled with deceit. There was never a real science crew, was there? And you followed some of us with hidden cameras, right?"

Pete flinched. "We ended up with the story you wanted. Don't get mad about the process now."

"I want to see what you have before this goes any further," she said, folding her arms over her chest and straightening.

"Now just wait a second. You aren't calling the shots here. Remember? It's in the contract that you and Seth signed as well as the releases from the whole town."

She didn't like much about Pete. From his fake smiles to his shallow conversation, he wasn't the brains behind the operation. And Elise needed to use that to her advantage right now.

She pointed at Mr. Willie. "You have no legal agreement with him."

"What?" Pete turned away, shooting daggers at the crew. "Where is Kate? She would know."

"We can wait for her to confirm," Elise rushed to add. "Or we can calm down and work out a compromise." She was bluffing. Big time. Only Pete wasn't smart enough to realize. As long as no one who knew her came near, she wouldn't be given up.

"What compromise? You don't want the shark story? You want the town to look like it's full of lunatics? Should I just go back to the reality TV footage? Or perhaps I do owe the Prims a visit to jail." Pete arched a brow and held her stare with a dead-eyed gaze of his own.

Elise held his gaze. She wouldn't shrink or show any reaction. "Why not call the *Sins of the Father* Podcast crew while you're at it? You'll get a very rambling, unbelievable story. You won't get good television."

Pete broke away first, shaking his head. "What do you want?"

"Let's go back to the museum with Mr. Willie. Let's have him sign a contract that also assures him you will not press any charges in exchange for his appearance. And I want you to be sure to include the unknown percentage of DNA in the documentary. That is the only fact you actually uncovered. Leave it in and keep the story open-ended."

"Why? To spare your boy toy's feelings?" Pete asked. "We've caught plenty on our cameras of your interactions. You might be cool as ice with everyone else. Not him. He's your weakness."

*No, he's my strength.* She realized she could dig deep and do for him what she never could for herself. Advocating for him was about the most illogical reason of all. Love.

She loved Seth deeply. Maybe she had spent her time worrying over how that looked to the outside world. Maybe she had wasted precious moments she could never get back. But with any luck, she could move forward. "You'll find we close ranks pretty quickly around here. And we don't like to live by absolutes. There is room for more than one monster in the lake. That's all I'm saying. We've had our fair share of extraordinary occurrences in this town. The community has come back stronger from each one."

"Fine." Pete spat on the ground and stuck out his hand. "Let's get going. I don't want to waste any more sunlight or any more time." He whistled and spun around.

"Mr. Willie, I'm sorry to ask you to do this," she said.

"No, I'm the one who owes everyone an apology. I never thought it would get this far out of hand. I think Patrick likes Seth. He's only ever surfaced for him and me. Do you think they'll let Patrick stay?"

Elise held her tongue. According to Seth, he'd never seen Patrick before. She wasn't sure if Seth would throw his support behind the shark instead of his mosasaurus. "I wish I had an answer. We have to let the DNR make those decisions. And the fish and wildlife team. But if there has been no significant disruption to the ecosystem—no one realized a shark was in the water—I can't imagine why they'd trap him."

"Thanks, I hope you're right. That made me feel better. I suppose I do feel lighter, too, now that my secret is out in the open. You should, too."

"What's my secret?" she asked.

"The lad." Mr. Willie winked and turned away. "Get me the paper, like Elise says. And I'll do it."

She pressed her lips together, not trusting a response. Seth made her the best version of herself. Around him, she was softer, better, kinder. She didn't want to lose that or him. Could she somehow have it all? Did she deserve it?

A figure jogged through the forest. "ELISE."

Her hand dropped to her back pocket, confirming the presence of her phone. Tim had tracked her down. If he caused a scene, he might ruin everything. Not that she hadn't already done that herself.

She decided to reach him first and put distance between herself and the nosy crew. "Hey." She stopped several yards away from where the crew packed up their equipment. "Good news, Soupy is real. It's actually a long story, but—"

"Why weren't you picking up my calls? I've been trying you all day."

"Oh, right. I'm sorry."

"I was serious when I told you I wanted to be kept in the loop. What happened with your meeting? What's going on here?" He shook his head. "I had great news to share with you. I've received so many inquiries about fundraising that I created a special account on the website for your foundation. And guess what, it's almost at your goal."

Her eyes bugged. "What?" she gasped.

"That's why I was calling." He ran a hand through his hair. "I don't know how to make you trust that I want to be your teammate. Please let me and others in."

"You're right." Her voice cracked. Tears stung her eyes. While she'd been busy trying to tackle an out-of-control situation, she'd relinquished her tight hold on her goal. And others had come through. All she'd succeeded in doing was pushing away the one person she cared about. The one person who looked at her and saw her. She wiped at her eyes.

"Okay. Good. Tough mayor act over." He scrubbed a hand over his face. "Soupy is real? Like really real? Seth must be over the moon."

"He isn't. But...he will be." She smiled.

# Chapter Nineteen

Seth wasn't a coward. He reminded himself of that fact as he did the brave thing and approached the museum again an hour later. Maybe this didn't prove his strength of character, but his weakness.

When he'd gotten the text from Pete, he'd wanted to delete it. Or better yet, chuck his phone into the lake. His conversation with Ashley only solidified that he had to prove his theory correct. Mr. Willie's pet wasn't Seth's Soupy. Something lurked out in the deep waters near the Timber Triangle. Molly and Grant's firsthand experience should be enough to cast doubt on what the documentary would present as the truth. He'd been down before, but he wasn't out. And he wouldn't be kicked like a dog by the TV producers. He refused to march back with his chin tucked to his chest to be filmed as they attempted to prove him wrong about what he'd searched for his whole life.

When the next alert from Elise arrived, he'd caved. He could have kicked himself for his reaction and the instant capitulation. As much as he wanted to stay away, he couldn't. He loved her. He'd probably always see her and smile and want more than the friendship they had. She didn't believe him. She accepted the fake answer and hurt him in the process. But he still couldn't keep his distance.

As he neared the log cabin, he didn't see her. His heart stuttered like he'd been rebooted. He wanted to see her and give them a chance to get back to where they had been. If they'd never be more, he'd have to accept that because the other option of not having her in his life was too much to bear. But perhaps the universe had given him a small mercy for good behavior. He needed time and a little bit of space to pull himself together and not be a lovesick fool eager for whatever scraps she threw him. He strolled inside, scanning the museum and hoping for a moment alone. At the back window, he spotted the familiar interview setup.

As the makeup artist touched up Pete, Mr. Willie squirmed on the chair next to him.

Seth studied Mr. Willie for the first time ever. The groundskeeper was in constant motion. Seth couldn't remember a time Mr. Willie hadn't been prowling and scowling. As a child, Seth had been intimidated by the man and his gruff voice and scruffy beard. But now?

Mr. Willie's dark hair had turned silver long ago. In his mid-sixties, he stooped more than he stood tall. His wrinkled skin softened the steady gaze. Overall, time had humanized him. On the tall chair, he looked almost vulnerable, like a strong breeze might blow him over.

"Mr. Boyd?" A female voice asked.

With a start, Seth turned toward the door. "Hi, Kate."

"I'm glad you're here." The producer smiled, but the expression was tense, and she didn't meet his gaze.

"I had to be." He kept his voice flat, not eager to betray the nerves twisting his stomach. "It's my story." *And Dad's.* Seth drew in a steadying breath. He needed a cool head. That's what Elise would advise. But questions danced on his tongue, and he couldn't keep quiet. "Was any of your production real? Were you tricking me the whole time?" he murmured, not eager for his voice to be picked up by any mics and recorded for posterity.

"We conducted research of the lake, as promised," Kate replied smoothly. "We had other angles, too."

"Who tipped you off about Mr. Willie?" Seth asked.

"No one. That was luck. We'd learned about the murky inheritance of the inn and the explosion last summer. A little more digging uncovered the underhanded lawyer." Kate lifted a shoulder. "We didn't go after the salacious angle. We could have."

Seth folded his arms over his chest. If she expected a thank you, she'd misjudged him.

"Learning Mr. Willie's secret was all thanks to luck and timing," Kate said. "Right place, right time."

"And you'd already turned the cameras off?" Seth asked.

"We didn't need to waste the time or money."

Seth wanted answers to so many other questions. He'd settle for clarity on one point. "Did you go to LA? At all? Or were you stalking Mr. Willie?"

"We had business." Kate sniffed, picking at imaginary lint on her shoulder like she'd grown bored of him. "But a few of the crew were given specific instructions to follow close behind Mr. Willie and keep tabs on him without his awareness of what we were doing."

Seth sighed. "There is still a mystery in the water. The unaccounted-for DNA. What will you do with that?" He persisted for Dad's sake.

"Our documentary has its conclusion. I suppose you'll chase the unknown." Kate pulled a sticker out of her coat pocket and flashed the cartoon image of Soupy. "Keep selling these. They're adorable."

"Why was I asked to be here? If you're developing your own climax to my story, you don't need me."

"I wanted to run something by you." She reached inside the tote on her shoulder and pulled out a stack of stapled papers and extended it.

He crossed towards her and accepted the stack, frowning. "What's this?"

"A draft of the voice-over narration," she said. "Let us know what you think. Come outside if you want to stay for Mr. Willie's interview."

He shook his head. Elise wasn't here, and he really didn't want to stay for the confession. Mr. Willie wasn't on trial and shouldn't feel like he faced an inquisition. "Thanks for this. I think I'll head back to the inn."

She nodded and left.

He wanted to ask if she'd seen Elise. He rolled up the papers into a cylinder and held it like a flashlight. Would it illuminate what he should do next? In all honesty, he realized his response might have been too sensitive. Soupy had become more than his myth. Soupy had become his life's guiding principle. Hearing that he was wrong had been a shock. Before he had time to process the information, he reacted to her relief and lashed out. Ashley had said her ghost was fake until it became real. Didn't the universe need to constantly assert its balance? Wouldn't it make sense for his real to become fake?

He glanced outside the window again.

The makeup artist had left, and a bright light shone on the men in chairs.

Seth didn't want to stay for this. He exited the log cabin and got into his car, glad he'd made the effort to get his vehicle for a quick escape. He drove out of the gravel lot and onto the road, stopping only when he reached the inn's parking lot.

He didn't head inside. Instead, he made his way around the side of the building, across the lawn, over the little bridge, and around the lighthouse to sit on a newly installed bench overlooking the water.

He didn't know if he wanted to be alone or not. This was his perfect compromise. In a few steps, he could have company.

The papers in his back pocket burned through his jeans. He unfurled the cylinder, flattening the curled sheets on his lap.

*"We came to Loon Lake,"* he read aloud, *"with a preconceived narrative. Like many Americans, we'd heard the touching Father-Son story that seemed both larger than life and impossibly personal. Who doesn't want to believe in mysteries? We all search for magic. But we were impressed from the start by not only Seth Boyd's absolute dedication to the myth and his encounters with the creature, but also with the town's unwavering encouragement. Was it all a joke everyone was in on? Or were we missing something? Would we discover that the real monster lived inside the humans?*

*Over several months of living in town, we learned that it wasn't an either-or scenario. The community's commitment wasn't dependent on the truth of the story. We came to explore the way the stories we tell ourselves become our limiting beliefs. How we have a tendency to trap ourselves in the darkest places we'd want to avoid. Instead, we discovered the reverse was true. Sometimes the tall tales encourage us to step outside of our experiences and hope. Some narratives show us love.*

*We had a list of reasons for coming. And Soupy was—admittedly—at the bottom. But, miraculously, the story is true. There is a monster in Loon Lake. And while that might not be the creature we were sold, it is still pretty remarkable. More than anything, Loon Lake and the search for Soupy have shown us how—by focusing on the specific—we can unlock the best for everyone around us."*

Seth heaved an exhale and swiped at his eye. "I'm sorry, Dad. We won't be a legacy. But maybe that's okay."

He lifted his gaze to the water, the smooth surface barely rippling. "You'll live on in me. For as long as I'm able."

Footsteps sounded on the bridge.

He turned his neck and watched a slim figure round the lighthouse. In the late afternoon sunlight, Elise's skin glowed. She was perfect and totally out of reach.

"Hey, can we chat?" Elise asked.

He stood and motioned to the bench with the papers. "Sure."

She brushed past him with her shoulder as she took her seat. "Oh, you read it?"

"You know what this is?"

She nodded. "I do." She sighed. "I'm glad the lighthouse was rebuilt. This view is spectacular. Who knew?"

*Misdirection?* The talk with Ashley replayed in his mind, filling him once again with sadness and fear. He couldn't turn off his feelings for her. He couldn't abandon his town either. So he was stuck with the unenviable position of trying to be her friend and never looking for more. He'd follow her lead. "Probably the Prims."

She chuckled. "Probably. I'm sorry for earlier. You were right, I do try to force life into manageable checklists. I didn't believe in Soupy. But I've always believed in you."

He nodded. "To be honest, I get the impression that's the town's general consensus."

"You do?"

He shrugged.

"I disagree. I think, I've come to learn that many people have had their own encounters over the years. You were right. But I'm sorry it was not in the way you imagined."

"I just... I let my dad down."

"You didn't. You couldn't."

"How can you be so sure?"

* * *

Elise was certain down to the marrow of her bones. She loved Seth, and he could never disappoint her. She was all in. "What did you think of that script?"

"It's really good. I guess Pete had more depth to him."

She rolled her eyes. "No, he's as shallow as he seems. Kate and I wrote that."

Seth widened his eyes. "Why?"

Elise filled her lungs, inhaling all the air she could to power her through. At least she was seated, so she didn't have to worry about collapsing. "Because it's true. You gave this town something more than anyone else ever has. You are incredible."

He didn't move.

She turned towards him, her knees bumping into his. "I'm sorry that I've struggled to believe in Soupy. But understand that I have always believed in you."

"Why?"

"Because you're one of the only people to look at others and see the good. You always take the high road. You treat everyone with kindness and care. Maybe even those who don't deserve your good heart. Like me."

He bumped his knee against hers. "You've always been my friend."

"But I want more because I love you," she murmured.

Time stood still. The ripples on the water flattened. The clouds didn't waft. The breeze stopped.

She'd broken the world.

She shouldn't have said it. She was falling into a vast pit of nothing. And now she was oddly rooted in place, her limbs too heavy and useless to move.

He leaned close, resting a hand on her knee. "Good."

She stared at his mouth only inches away. "Good?"

"I'm glad you said it first. No take backs." His lips curved into a grin. "And I was right."

Elise hated surprises. She couldn't seem to avoid them lately. But what if, in the end, it was really her heart that turned out to be the most chaotic instrument of all? She loved Seth. She didn't care about what anyone thought. Life was too precious and short to waste on public opinion.

She looked into his green eyes, glittering like emeralds, and was utterly lost. "Right about what?"

He brushed the side of her face with his fingertips, a feather-light touch. "That love is magic and a miracle."

She leaned into his hand and, on impulse, kissed his palm. Her cheeks burned.

If he noticed, he didn't say. Instead, he reached for her with both hands and kissed her. Every other consideration slid away. She wouldn't care what anyone in town said. Grant could drive the tour boat by right now and wave. She somehow had earned the love of most caring soul in town. She wouldn't squander the precious gift with stupid outside opinions ever again.

She leaned forward, deepening the kiss.

He dropped his hands to her waist, pulling her onto his lap and kissing her like he had to for survival.

A low moan escaped from her throat. The reaction was primal, and he gripped her tighter.

A deep sound echoed off the lighthouse.

He broke away from the kiss, panting. "Maybe we should slow down."

"Worried your groans will destroy the new lighthouse?" she teased.

He arched a brow. "Me? You're the one moaning."

"I moaned a little." Her cheeks flushed, but she refused to

be embarrassed about her reaction. Not now that they had finally reached this point and never again.

"What was that sound then?"

She shook her head, too dazed to care about anything besides what a good kisser he was.

"No, listen," he murmured.

The rumble came again, bouncing off the stones.

She heard it above the pounding of her heart.

"Oh my, look! There!" He slid her off his lap, stood, and pointed across the lake.

The loss of his warmth was like being dunked in the icy water. But she didn't care. It was only a second of separation, and she knew they'd have forever. They were together, and she supported him. She joined him and squinted, rubbed her eyes, and narrowed her gaze.

A long, scaly body slithered through the water. It looked like a crocodile or something reptilian. How could that be? Soupy was a shark.

"I've got to record this," he said. He fumbled with his pockets.

"I'm sure they have eyes on this already." She raised a hand to shield her gaze. The dark scales made it hard to spot the creature. Should she call Patrick by name and see if he responded? Were they all to treat him like a pet now? She shuddered. Reaching out a hand to stroke his back seemed a surefire way to lose an appendage.

"I'm not taking any chances. I haven't seen Soupy this close to the surface in decades." He grabbed his phone and aimed his camera at the quickly moving object.

She grabbed her phone out of her pocket and hit the video call app with Kate. "Hey, are you guys getting this?"

"Soupy sighting?" Kate asked, tipping her head to the side. She angled the camera.

On the screen behind Kate, Mr. Willie fed the shark in the tiny pond.

"No, not that one," Elise murmured and flipped the camera to capture the surface of the lake. But whatever had been there had disappeared. Only a few ripples remained. The disturbance was too far away for the limited zoom capabilities.

"I'm not seeing anything," Kate said. "But you're going to want to listen to this. Is Seth there?"

Elise met Seth's gaze.

"He's gone," Seth murmured and shrugged.

"Yes, he's here. Hold on," Elise said. She tipped her head toward the bench.

Seth sat down, and Elise joined him.

"Okay, great," Kate said, angling her camera until Mr. Willie came into view.

"Patrick has cost me everything," Mr. Willie said, his voice slightly muffled from the distance to the phone. "When I first came to Loon Lake, I kept him in a little aquarium. But as time went on, I had to release him into the water. A growing lad needed room to swim. He was lonely. And continued to return to the little spring where I first set him free. Luckily, as groundskeeper, I had plenty of reason to trek around the property at all hours. I've fed him and kept him company over the years. He's my family." Mr. Willie sniffed.

Elise swiped at her lower lashes.

Seth wrapped an arm around her shoulder and hugged her.

She leaned her head against her shoulder. Everyone was getting their happily ever after.

"I had the chance to go home and take over the property that I grew up dreaming about for a family I've known forever," Mr. Willie continued, his voice slightly wistful. "Patrick means everything to me. I'll never leave him."

The camera flipped to selfie mode.

With a start, Elise straightened, coming out of Seth's embrace.

Kate widened her eyes. "We've got what we need here. We're going to wrap up production and head out tonight," she said. "Best of luck. We'll be in touch about the premiere."

"Okay, sounds good," Elise said the words by rote and ended the call.

"Poor Mr. Willie," Seth murmured.

"He's got to be sort of relieved to have the secret out. Ashley and Christopher won't keep him from the pond." She reached for Seth's hand and squeezed. "But now we know the truth," Elise said. "Soupy is still out there."

"10 percent unknown DNA, right?" Seth asked, smirking. "I'm not the only one to have seen him anymore."

She nodded. "You'll never be the only one ever again."

Seth leaned forward and pressed his lips against hers. She relaxed into the kiss.

The lake was big enough for more than one monster. The community was welcoming of all, even the mysterious and most definitely the prehistoric. And now she was the biggest believer of all.

Rachelle Paige Campbell writes contemporary romance novels filled with heart and hope. She believes love and laughter can change lives, and every story needs a happily ever after. Learn more at her website https://rachellepaigecampbell.com/

# About the Publisher

Harbor Lane Books, LLC is a US-based independent digital publisher of commercial fiction, non-fiction, and poetry.

Connect with Harbor Lane Books on their website (www. harborlanebooks.com) and social media @harborlanebooks.

facebook.com/harborlanebooks

x.com/harborlanebooks

instagram.com/harborlanebooks

bsky.app/profile/harborlanebooks.bsky.social

tiktok.com/@harborlanebooks

threads.com/harborlanebooks

youtube.com/harborlanebooks

pinterest.com/harborlanebooks